POKÉMON™

BLACK AND WHITE

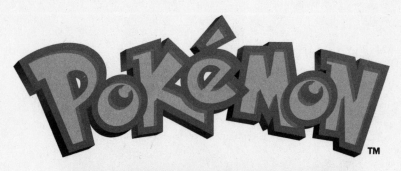

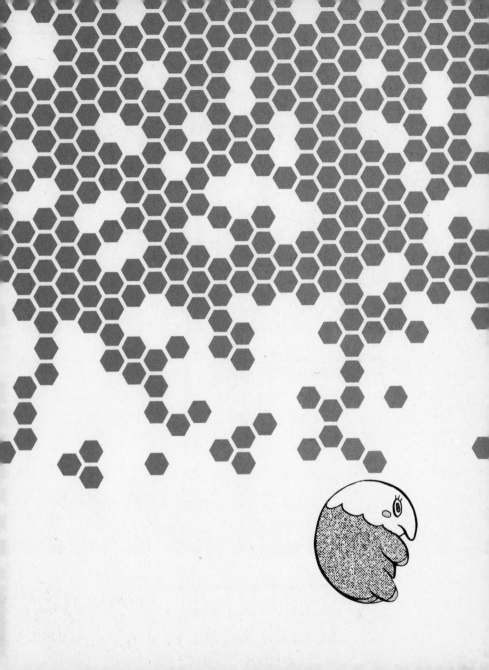

POKÉMON™

BLACK AND WHITE

VOL.19

Story by **HIDENORI KUSAKA**
Art by **SATOSHI YAMAMOTO**

Pokémon Black and White
Volume 19
Perfect Square Edition

Story by HIDENORI KUSAKA
Art by SATOSHI YAMAMOTO

© 2014 Pokémon.
© 1995–2014 Nintendo/Creatures Inc./GAME FREAK inc.
TM, ®, and character names are trademarks of Nintendo.
POCKET MONSTERS SPECIAL (Magazine Edition)
by Hidenori KUSAKA, Satoshi YAMAMOTO
© 1997 Hidenori KUSAKA, Satoshi YAMAMOTO
All rights reserved.
Original Japanese edition published by SHOGAKUKAN.
English translation rights in the United States of America, Canada, the United Kingdom,
Ireland, Australia and New Zealand arranged with SHOGAKUKAN.

English Adaptation / Bryant Turnage
Translation / Tetsuichiro Miyaki
Touch-up & Lettering / Susan Daigle-Leach
Design / Fawn Lau
Editor / Annette Roman

Printed in the U.S.A.

Published by VIZ Media, LLC
P.O. Box 77010
San Francisco, CA 94107

10 9 8 7 6 5 4 3 2 1
First printing, December 2014

www.perfectsquare.com

www.viz.com

POKÉMON

BLACK AND WHITE

VOL.19

THE STORY THUS FAR!

Pokémon Trainer Black is exploring the mysterious Unova region with his brand-new Pokédex. Pokémon Trainer White runs a thriving talent agency for performing Pokémon. While traveling together, their paths cross with Team Plasma, a nefarious group that advocates releasing your Pokémon into the wild! Now Black and White are off on their own separate journeys of discovery...

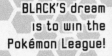

BLACK'S dream is to win the Pokémon League!

WHITE'S dream is to work in show biz... and now she's learning how to Pokémon Battle as well!

Black's Munna, MUSHA, helps him think clearly, but now Musha has left him!

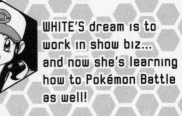

White's Tepig, GIGI, and Black's Emboar, BO, get along like peanut butter and jelly! But Gigi left White for another Trainer...

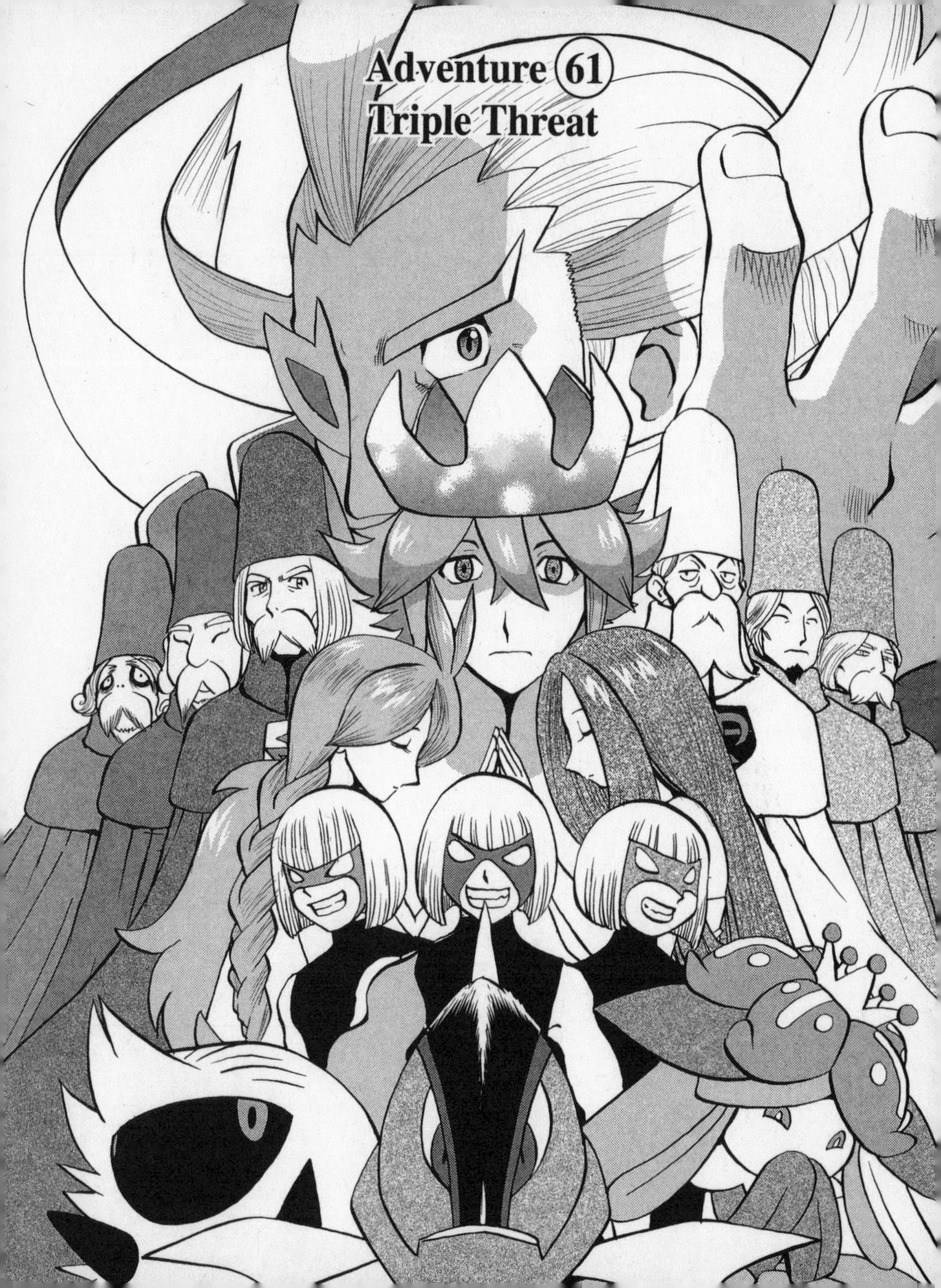
Adventure 61
Triple Threat

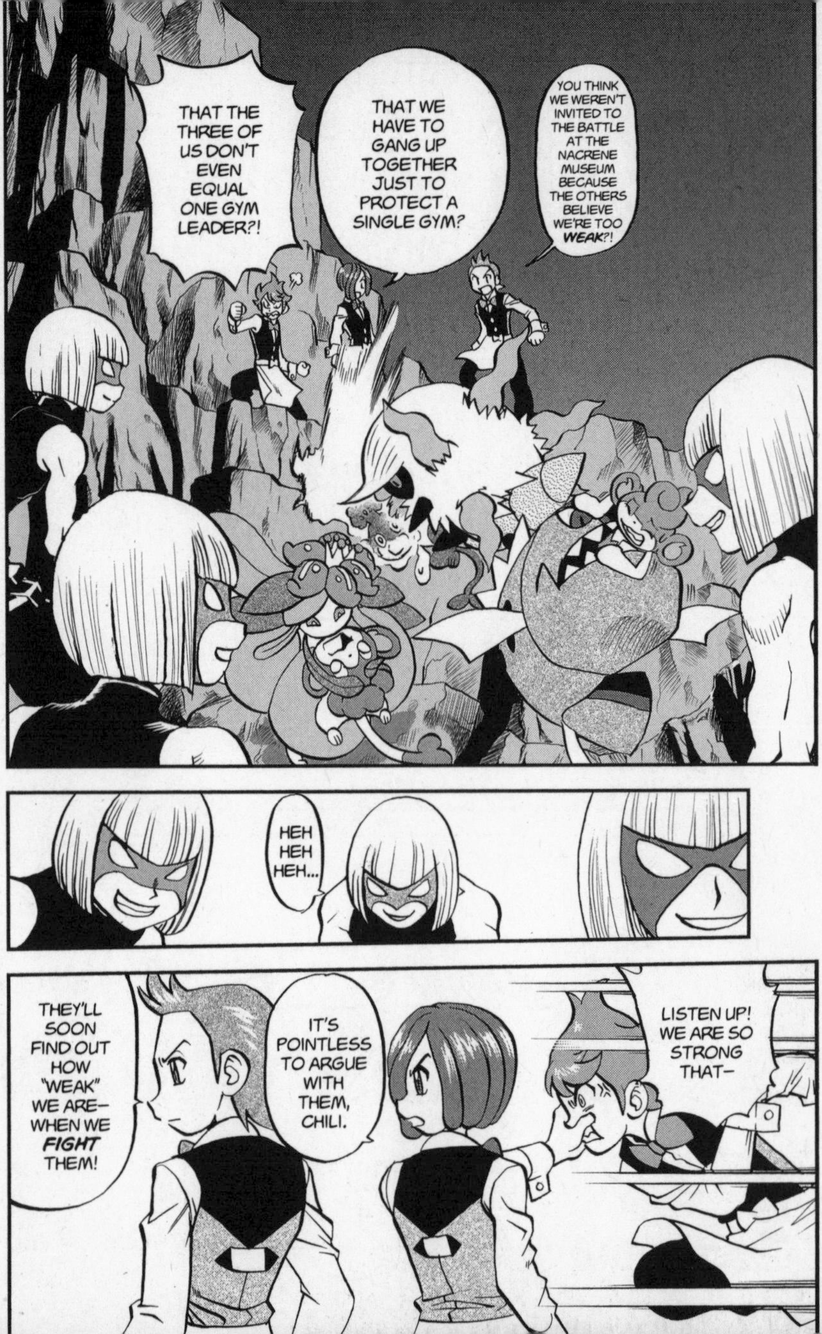
YOU THINK WE WEREN'T INVITED TO THE BATTLE AT THE NACRENE MUSEUM BECAUSE THE OTHERS BELIEVE WE'RE TOO ***WEAK***?!
THAT WE HAVE TO GANG UP TOGETHER JUST TO PROTECT A SINGLE GYM?
THAT THE THREE OF US DON'T EVEN EQUAL ONE GYM LEADER?!
HEH HEH HEH...
LISTEN UP! WE ARE SO STRONG THAT—
IT'S POINTLESS TO ARGUE WITH THEM, CHILI.
THEY'LL SOON FIND OUT HOW "WEAK" WE ARE—WHEN WE ***FIGHT*** THEM!

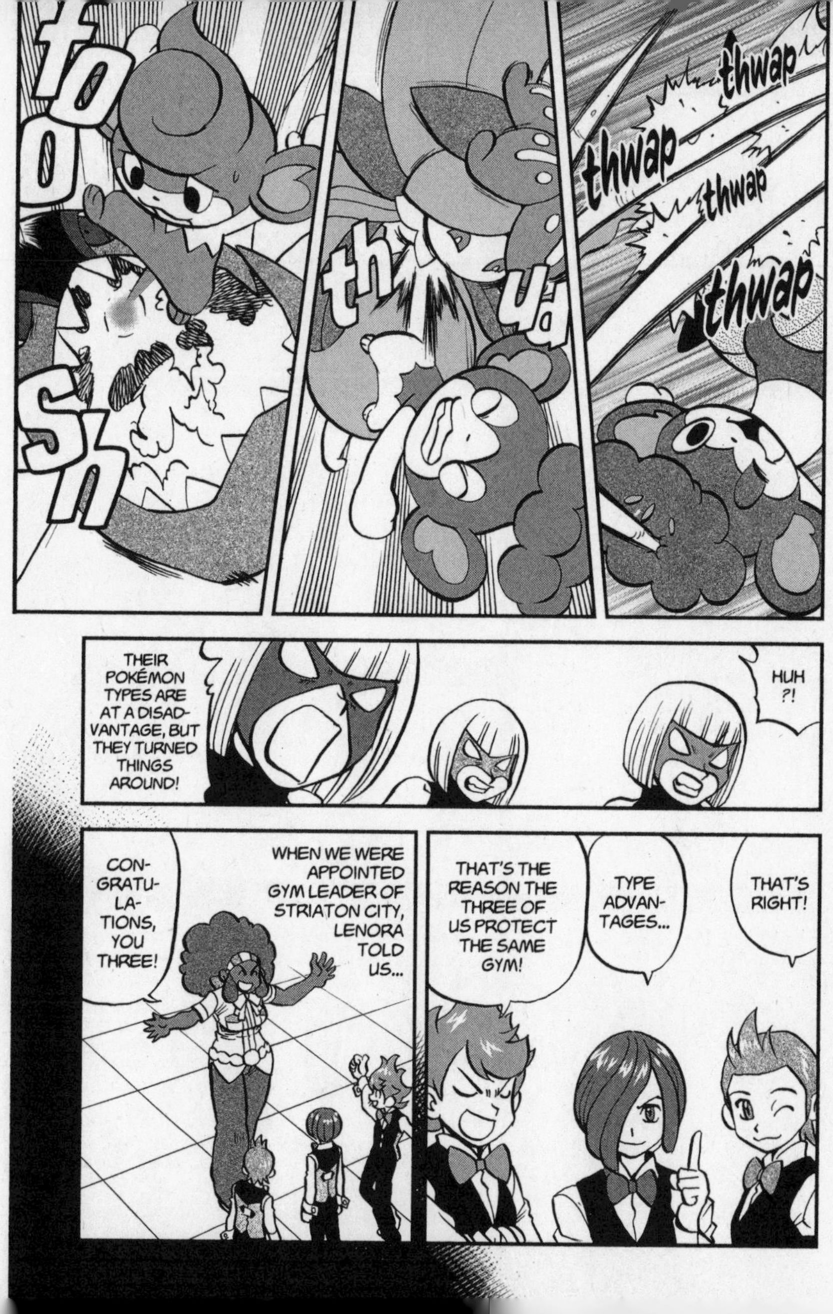
thwap
thwap
thwap
thwap
thud
toosh
HUH?!
THEIR POKÉMON TYPES ARE AT A DISADVANTAGE, BUT THEY TURNED THINGS AROUND!
THAT'S RIGHT!
TYPE ADVANTAGES...
THAT'S THE REASON THE THREE OF US PROTECT THE SAME GYM!
WHEN WE WERE APPOINTED GYM LEADER OF STRIATON CITY, LENORA TOLD US...
CONGRATULATIONS, YOU THREE!

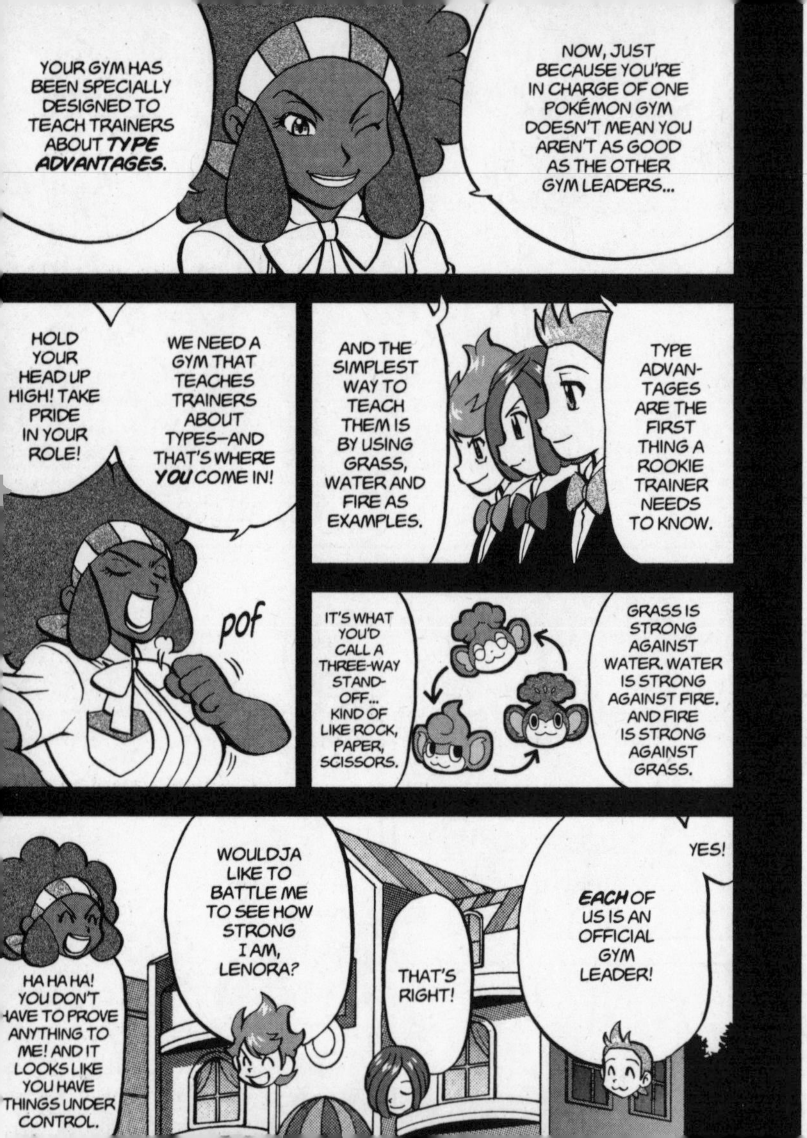
NOW, JUST BECAUSE YOU'RE IN CHARGE OF ONE POKÉMON GYM DOESN'T MEAN YOU AREN'T AS GOOD AS THE OTHER GYM LEADERS...
YOUR GYM HAS BEEN SPECIALLY DESIGNED TO TEACH TRAINERS ABOUT ***TYPE ADVANTAGES***.
TYPE ADVAN-TAGES ARE THE FIRST THING A ROOKIE TRAINER NEEDS TO KNOW.
AND THE SIMPLEST WAY TO TEACH THEM IS BY USING GRASS, WATER AND FIRE AS EXAMPLES.
GRASS IS STRONG AGAINST WATER. WATER IS STRONG AGAINST FIRE. AND FIRE IS STRONG AGAINST GRASS.
IT'S WHAT YOU'D CALL A THREE-WAY STAND-OFF... KIND OF LIKE ROCK, PAPER, SCISSORS.
WE NEED A GYM THAT TEACHES TRAINERS ABOUT TYPES—AND THAT'S WHERE ***YOU*** COME IN!
HOLD YOUR HEAD UP HIGH! TAKE PRIDE IN YOUR ROLE!
pof
YES!
EACH OF US IS AN OFFICIAL GYM LEADER!
THAT'S RIGHT!
WOULDJA LIKE TO BATTLE ME TO SEE HOW STRONG I AM, LENORA?
HA HA HA! YOU DON'T HAVE TO PROVE ANYTHING TO ME! AND IT LOOKS LIKE YOU HAVE THINGS UNDER CONTROL.

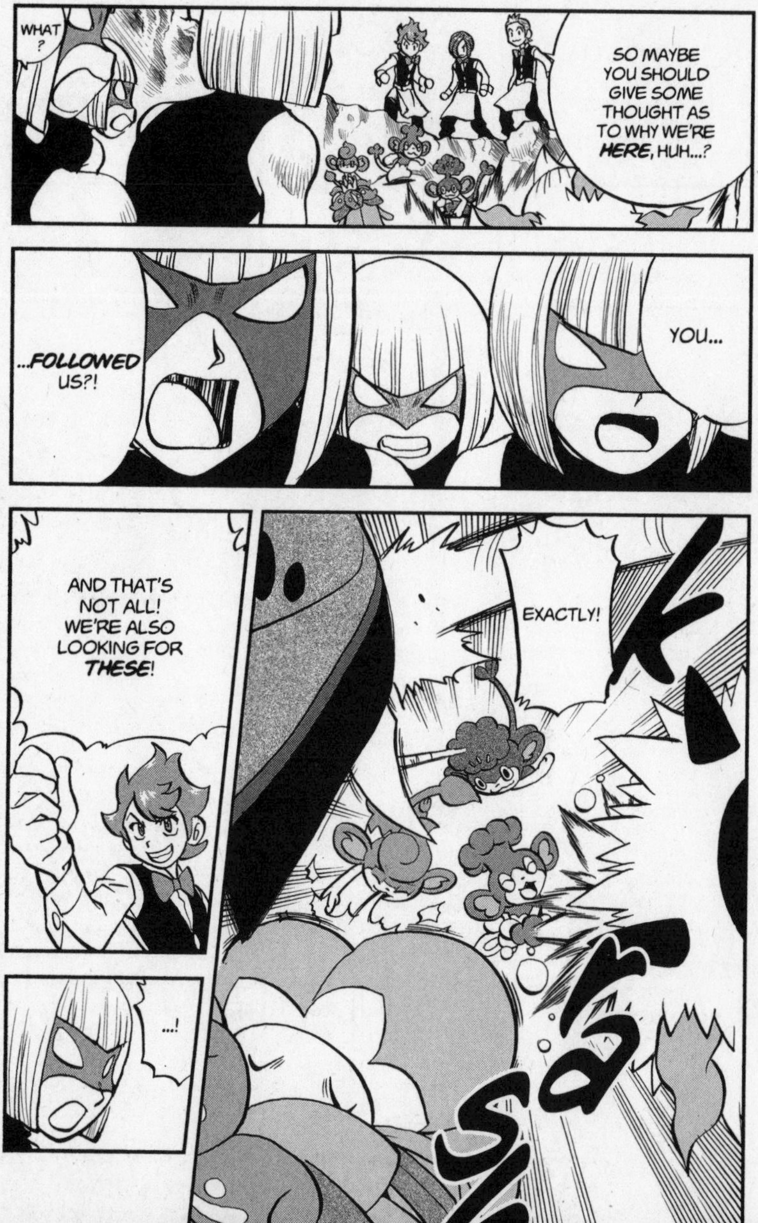
SO MAYBE YOU SHOULD GIVE SOME THOUGHT AS TO WHY WE'RE **HERE**, HUH...?
WHAT?
YOU...
...**FOLLOWED** US?!
EXACTLY!
AND THAT'S NOT ALL! WE'RE ALSO LOOKING FOR **THESE**!
...!

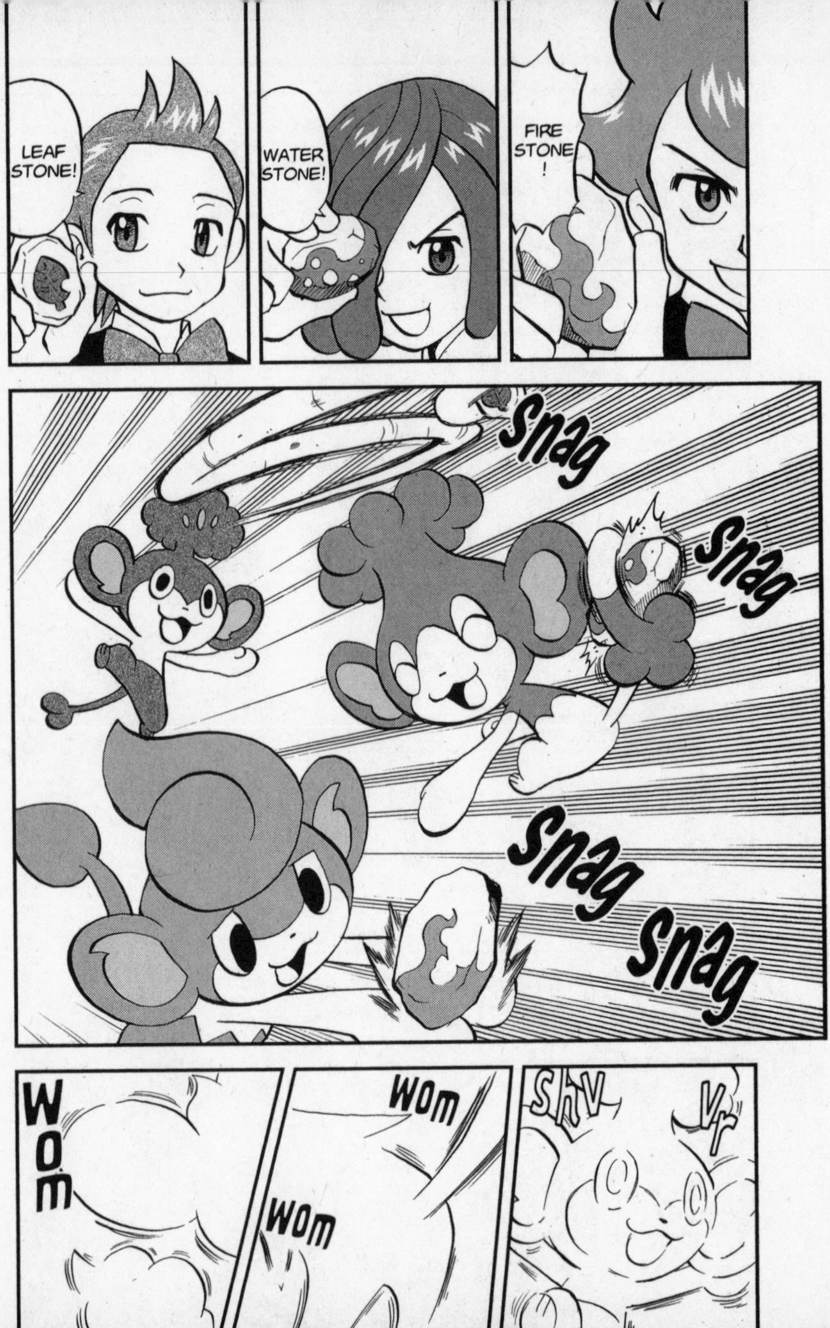
FIRE STONE!
WATER STONE!
LEAF STONE!
Snag
Snag
Snag
Snag
Vr
Shv
wom
wom
Wom

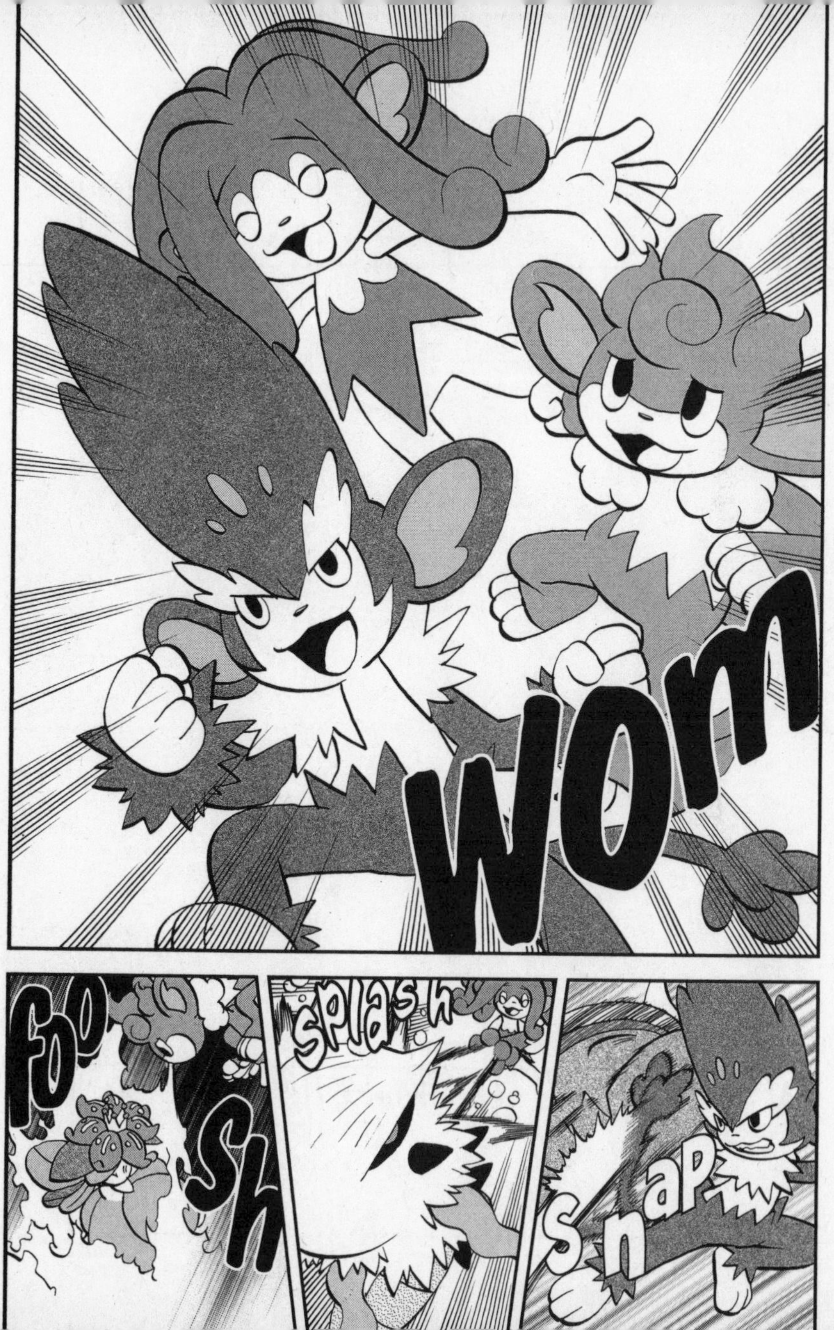
WOM
snap
splash
foosh

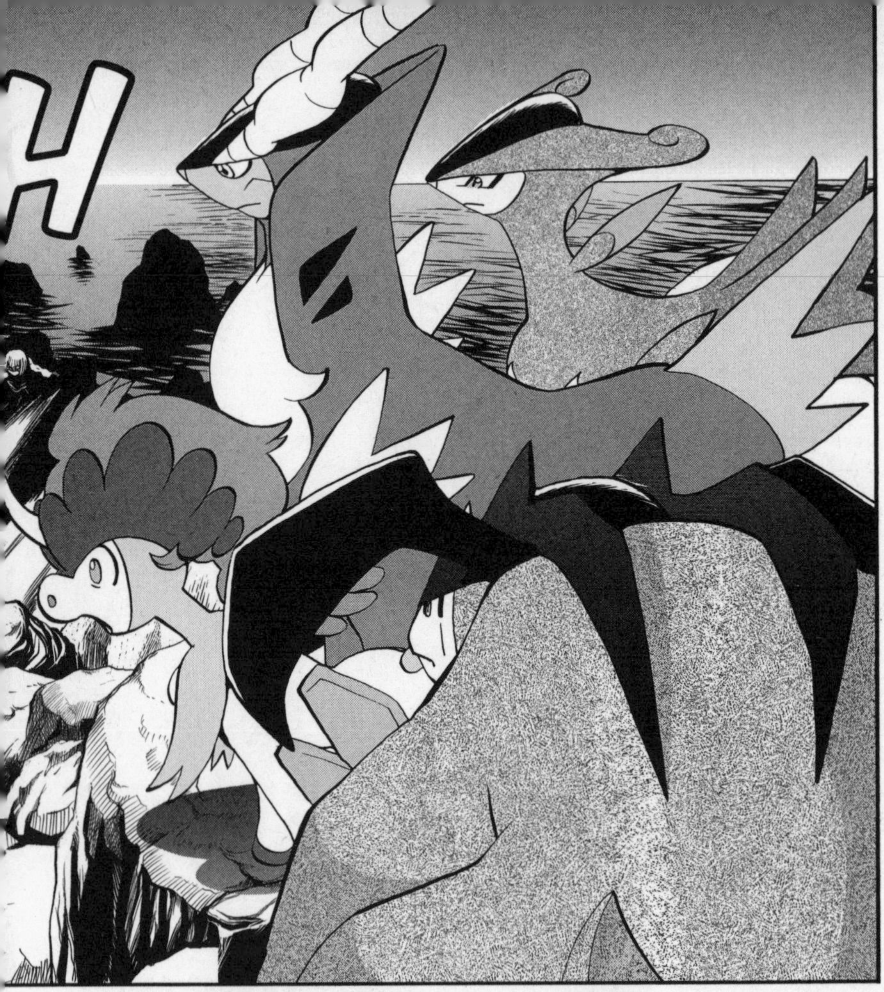
H

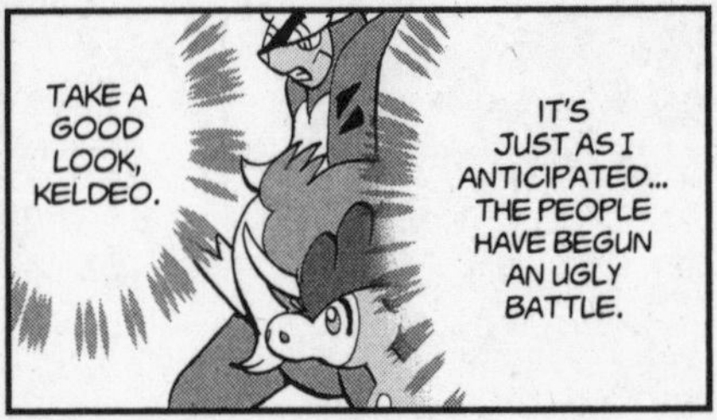
TAKE A GOOD LOOK, KELDEO.
IT'S JUST AS I ANTICIPATED... THE PEOPLE HAVE BEGUN AN UGLY BATTLE.

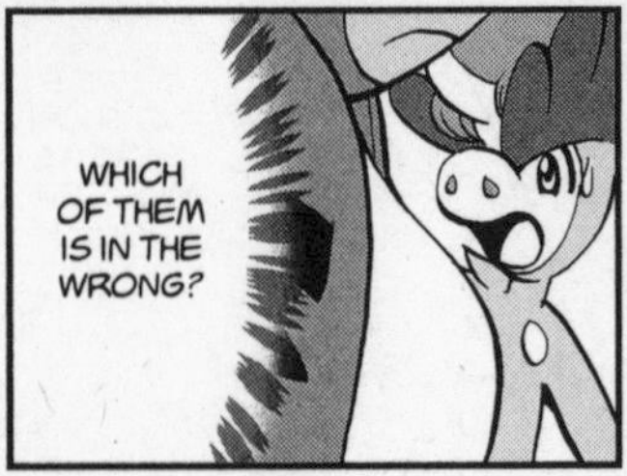
WHICH OF THEM IS IN THE WRONG?

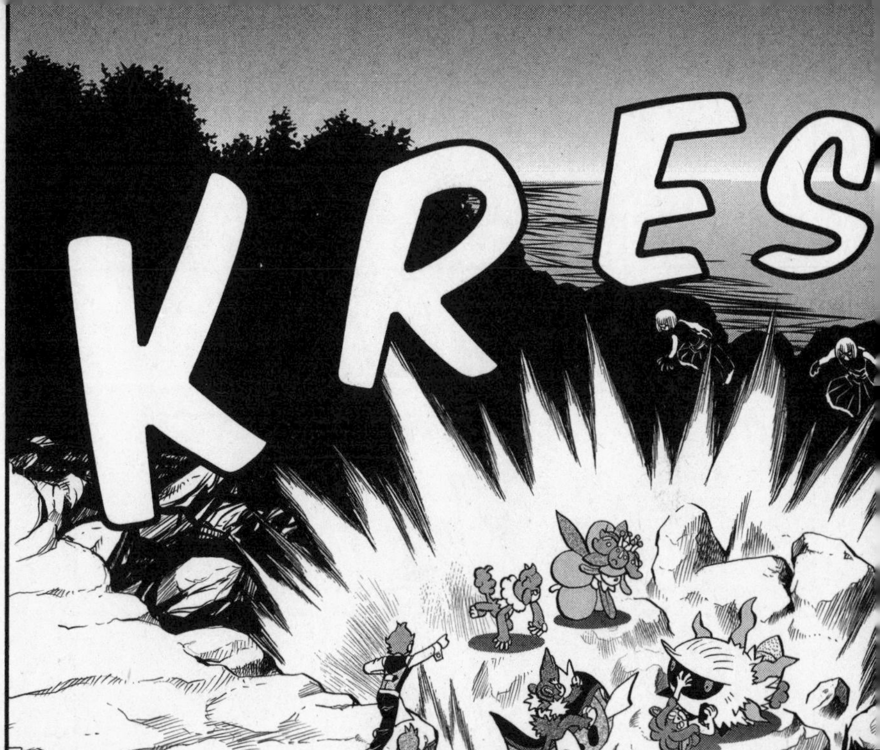
KRES

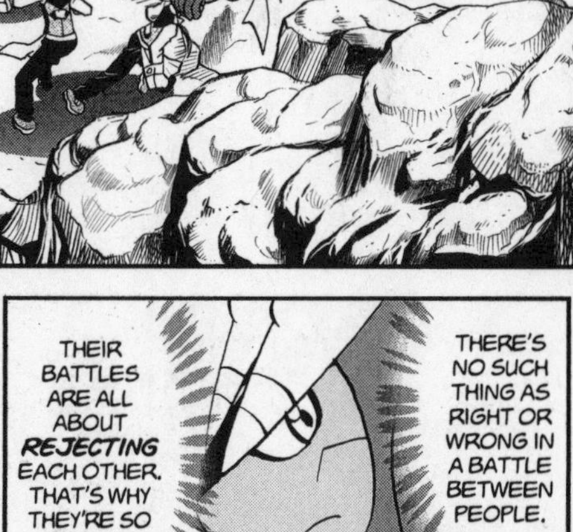
THERE'S NO SUCH THING AS RIGHT OR WRONG IN A BATTLE BETWEEN PEOPLE.
THEIR BATTLES ARE ALL ABOUT *REJECTING* EACH OTHER. THAT'S WHY THEY'RE SO HORRIBLE.

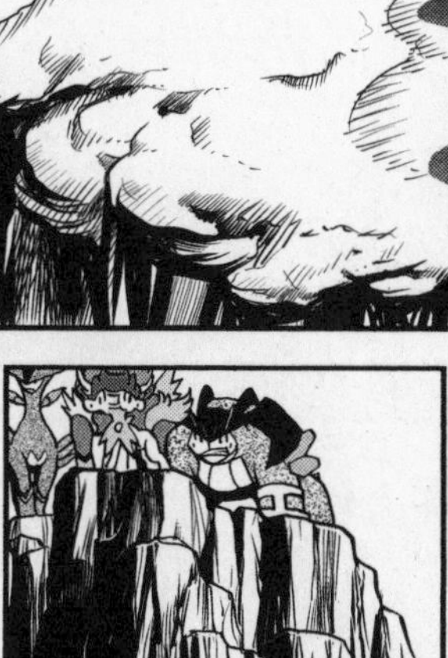

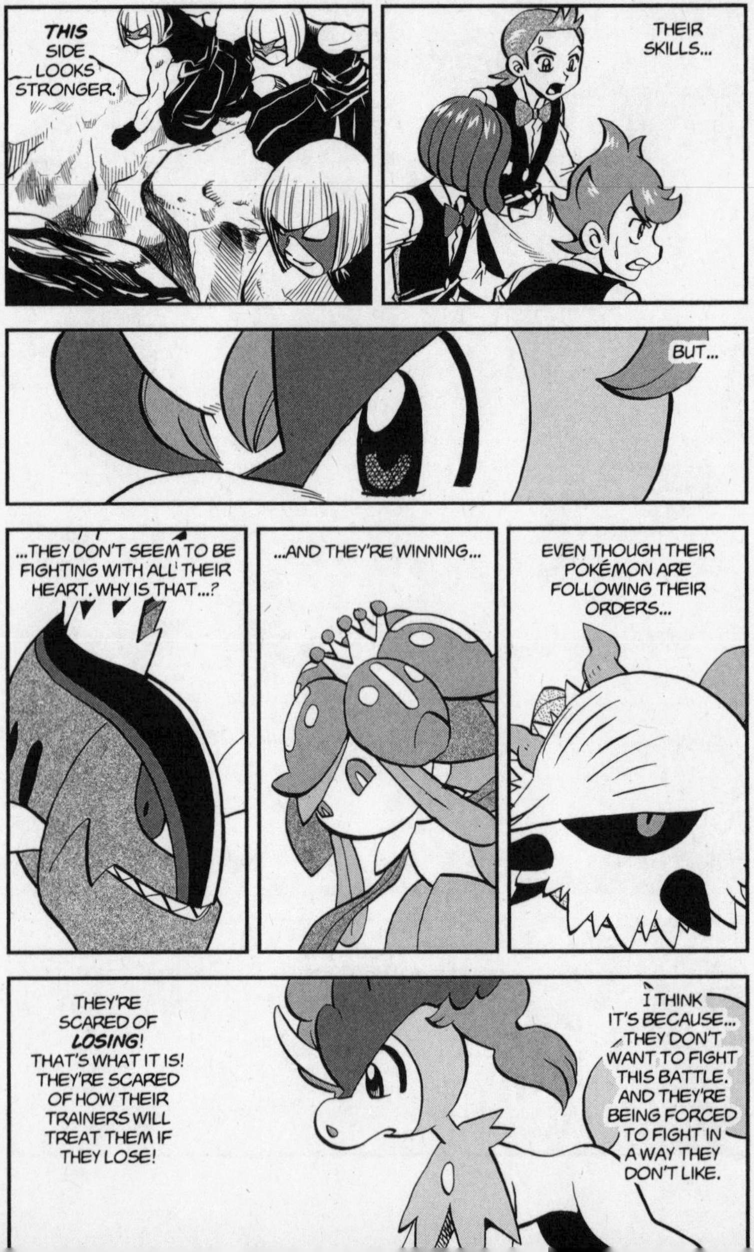
THEIR SKILLS...
THIS SIDE LOOKS STRONGER.
BUT...
EVEN THOUGH THEIR POKÉMON ARE FOLLOWING THEIR ORDERS...
...AND THEY'RE WINNING...
...THEY DON'T SEEM TO BE FIGHTING WITH ALL THEIR HEART. WHY IS THAT...?
I THINK IT'S BECAUSE... THEY DON'T WANT TO FIGHT THIS BATTLE. AND THEY'RE BEING FORCED TO FIGHT IN A WAY THEY DON'T LIKE.
THEY'RE SCARED OF ***LOSING***! THAT'S WHAT IT IS! THEY'RE SCARED OF HOW THEIR TRAINERS WILL TREAT THEM IF THEY LOSE!

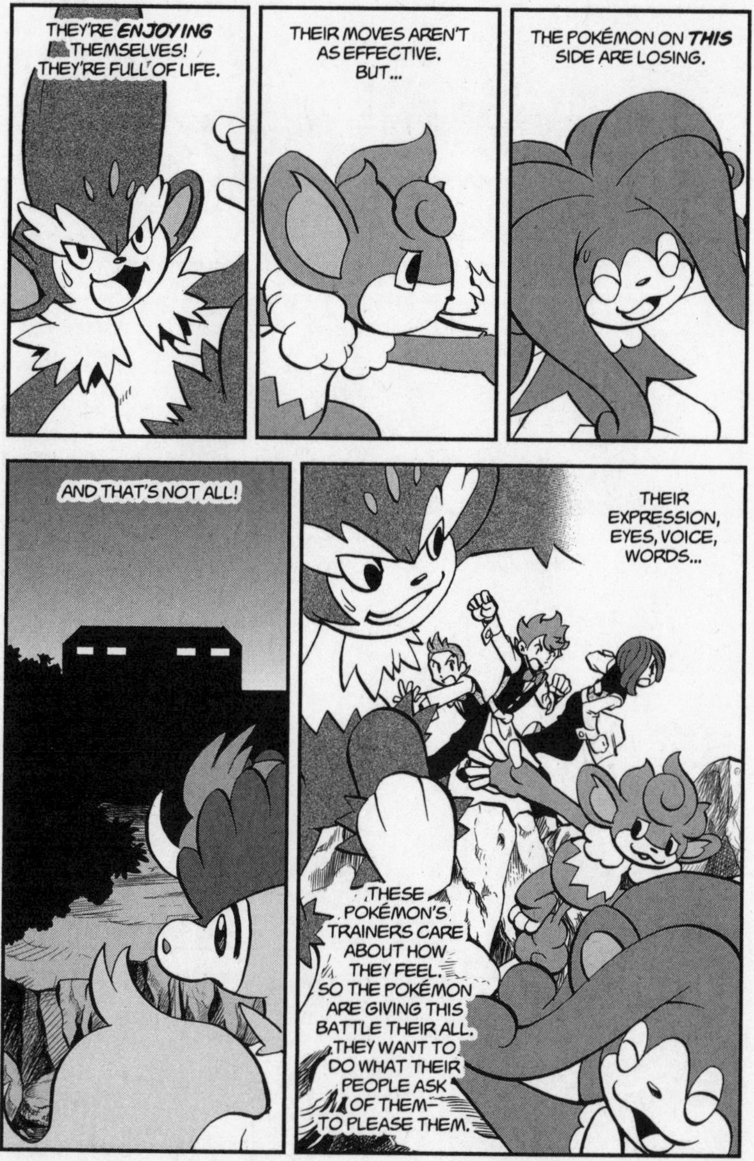
THE POKÉMON ON THIS SIDE ARE LOSING.
THEIR MOVES AREN'T AS EFFECTIVE. BUT...
THEY'RE ENJOYING THEMSELVES! THEY'RE FULL OF LIFE.
THEIR EXPRESSION, EYES, VOICE, WORDS...
THESE POKÉMON'S TRAINERS CARE ABOUT HOW THEY FEEL. SO THE POKÉMON ARE GIVING THIS BATTLE THEIR ALL. THEY WANT TO DO WHAT THEIR PEOPLE ASK OF THEM— TO PLEASE THEM.
AND THAT'S NOT ALL!

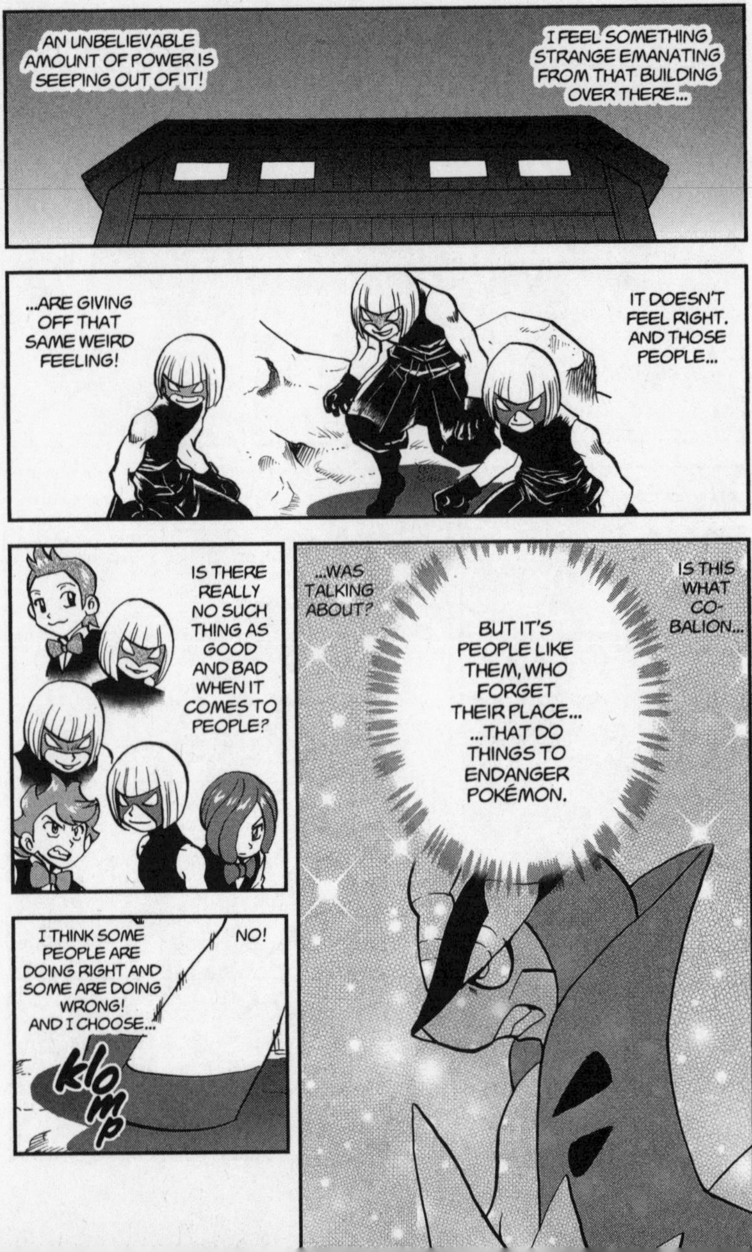
I FEEL SOMETHING STRANGE EMANATING FROM THAT BUILDING OVER THERE...
AN UNBELIEVABLE AMOUNT OF POWER IS SEEPING OUT OF IT!
IT DOESN'T FEEL RIGHT. AND THOSE PEOPLE...
...ARE GIVING OFF THAT SAME WEIRD FEELING!
IS THIS WHAT CO-BALION...
...WAS TALKING ABOUT?
BUT IT'S PEOPLE LIKE THEM, WHO FORGET THEIR PLACE... ...THAT DO THINGS TO ENDANGER POKÉMON.
IS THERE REALLY NO SUCH THING AS GOOD AND BAD WHEN IT COMES TO PEOPLE?
NO!
I THINK SOME PEOPLE ARE DOING RIGHT AND SOME ARE DOING WRONG! AND I CHOOSE...
klomp

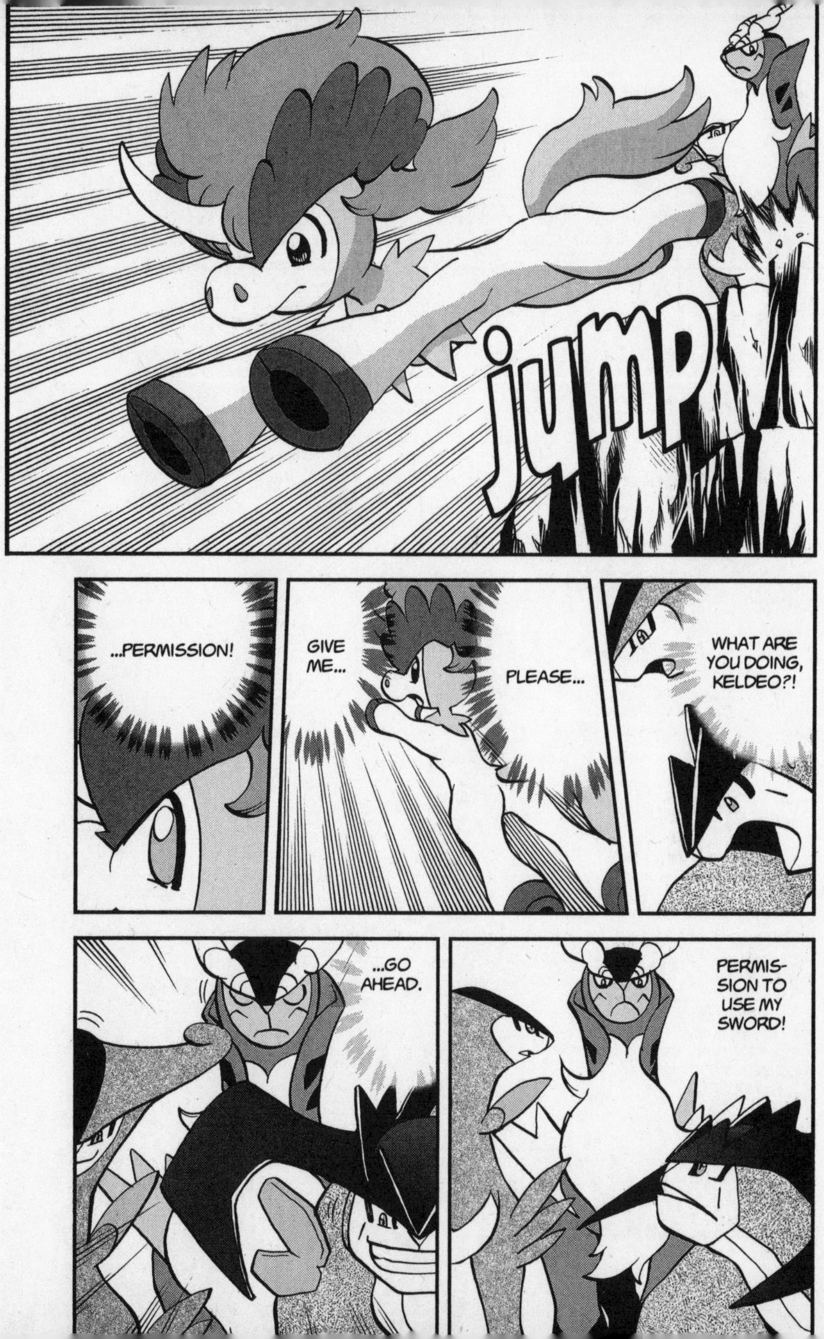
jump
WHAT ARE YOU DOING, KELDEO?!
PLEASE...
GIVE ME...
...PERMISSION!
PERMIS-SION TO USE MY SWORD!
...GO AHEAD.

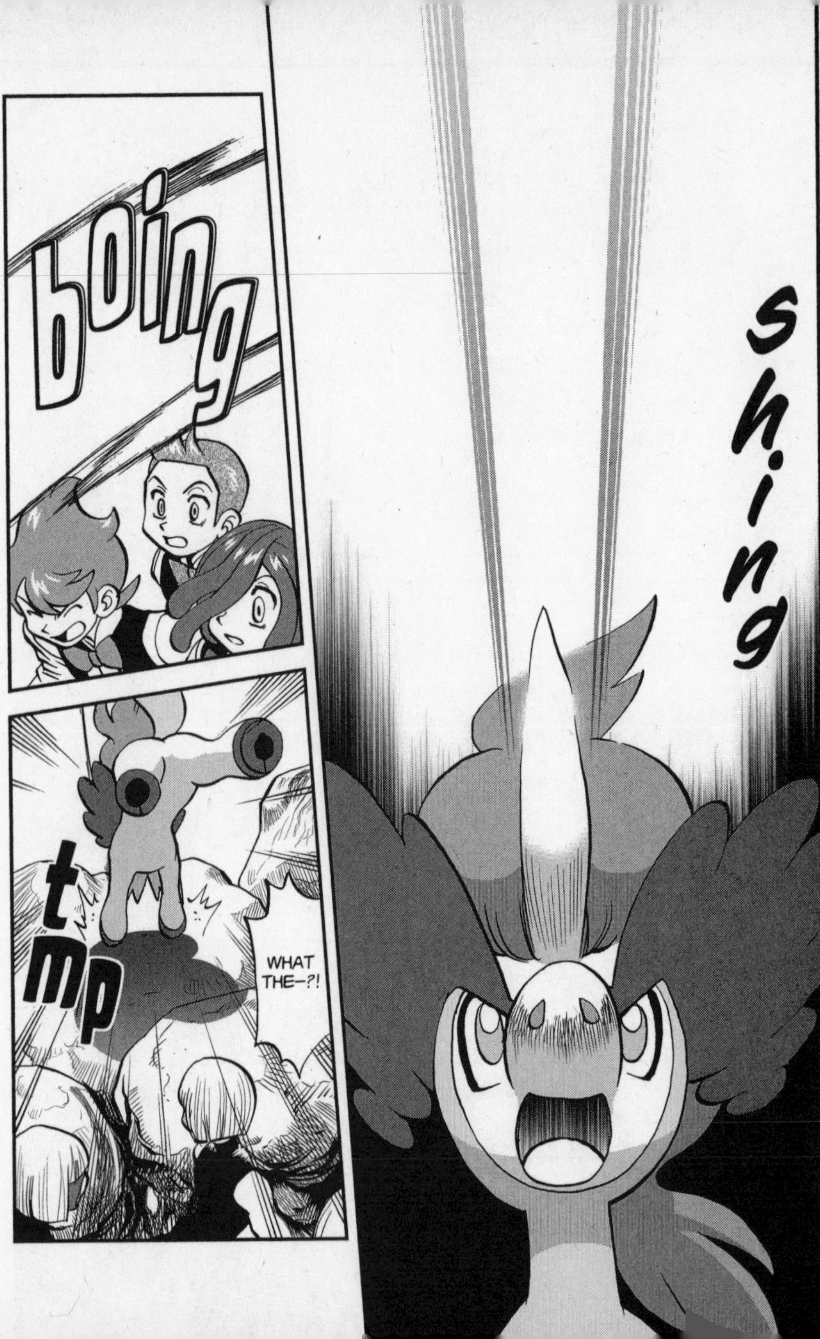
shing
boing
tmp
WHAT THE-?!

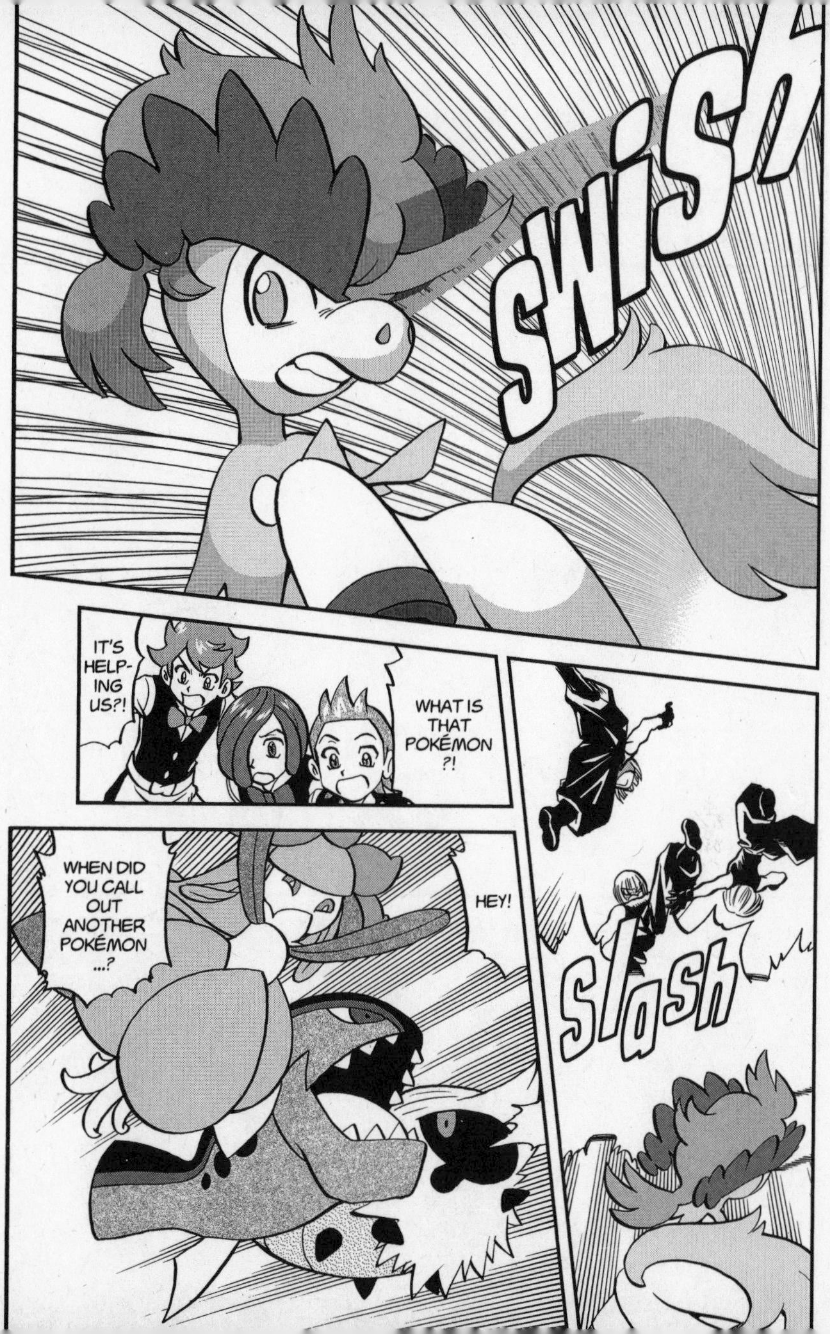
SWISH
SLASH
WHAT IS THAT POKÉMON?!
IT'S HELPING US?!
HEY!
WHEN DID YOU CALL OUT ANOTHER POKÉMON...?

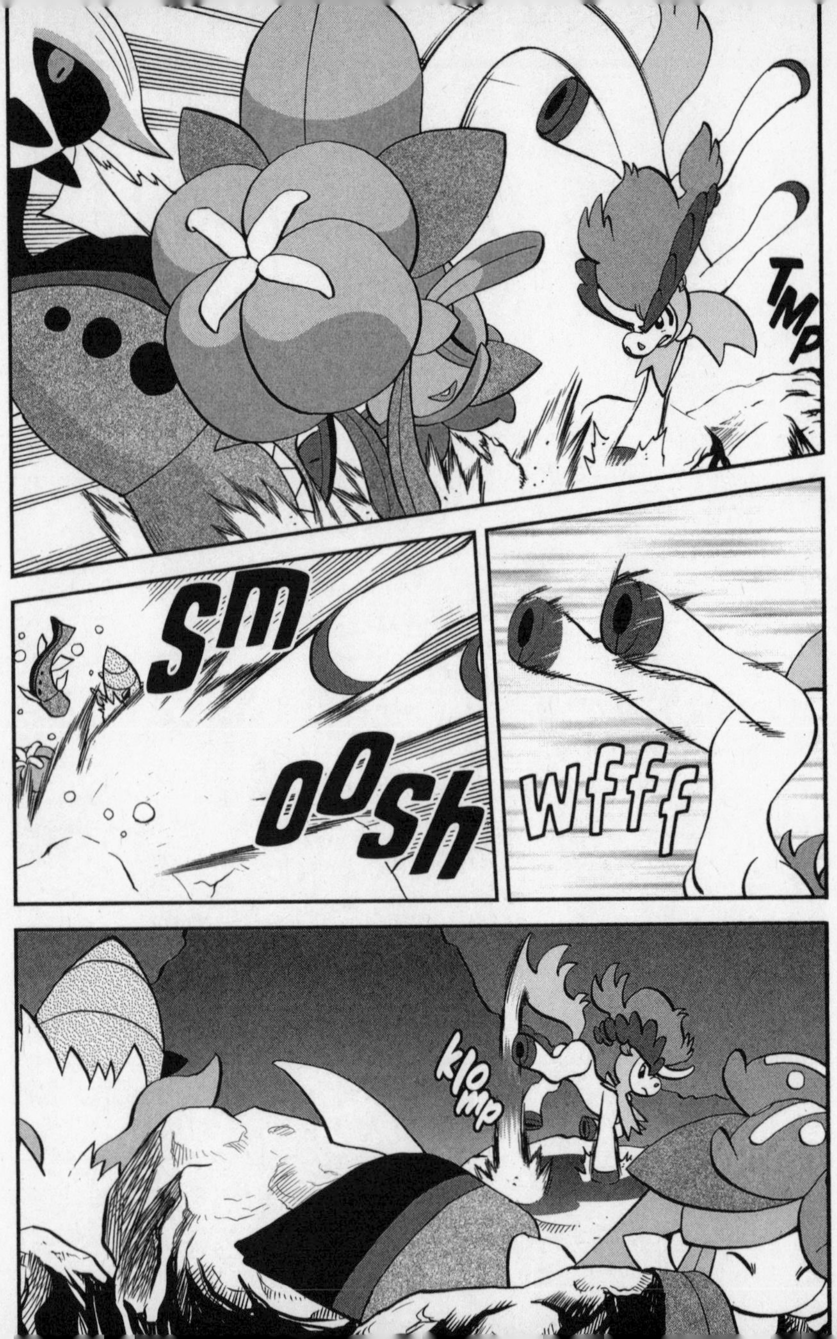
TMP
wfff
SMOOSH
klomp

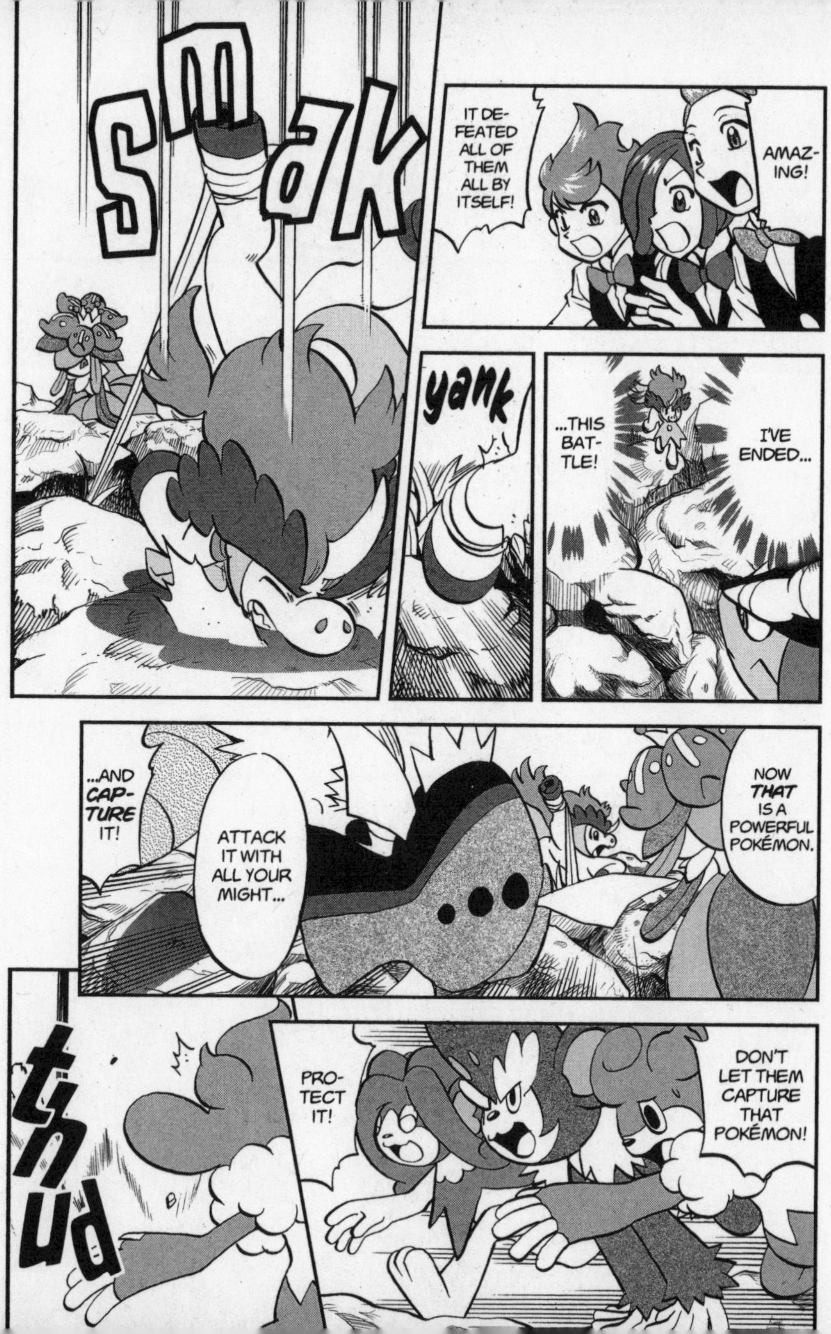
AMAZ-ING!
IT DE-FEATED ALL OF THEM ALL BY ITSELF!
I'VE ENDED...
...THIS BAT-TLE!
yank
smak
NOW THAT IS A POWERFUL POKÉMON.
ATTACK IT WITH ALL YOUR MIGHT...
...AND CAP-TURE IT!
DON'T LET THEM CAPTURE THAT POKÉMON!
PRO-TECT IT!
thud

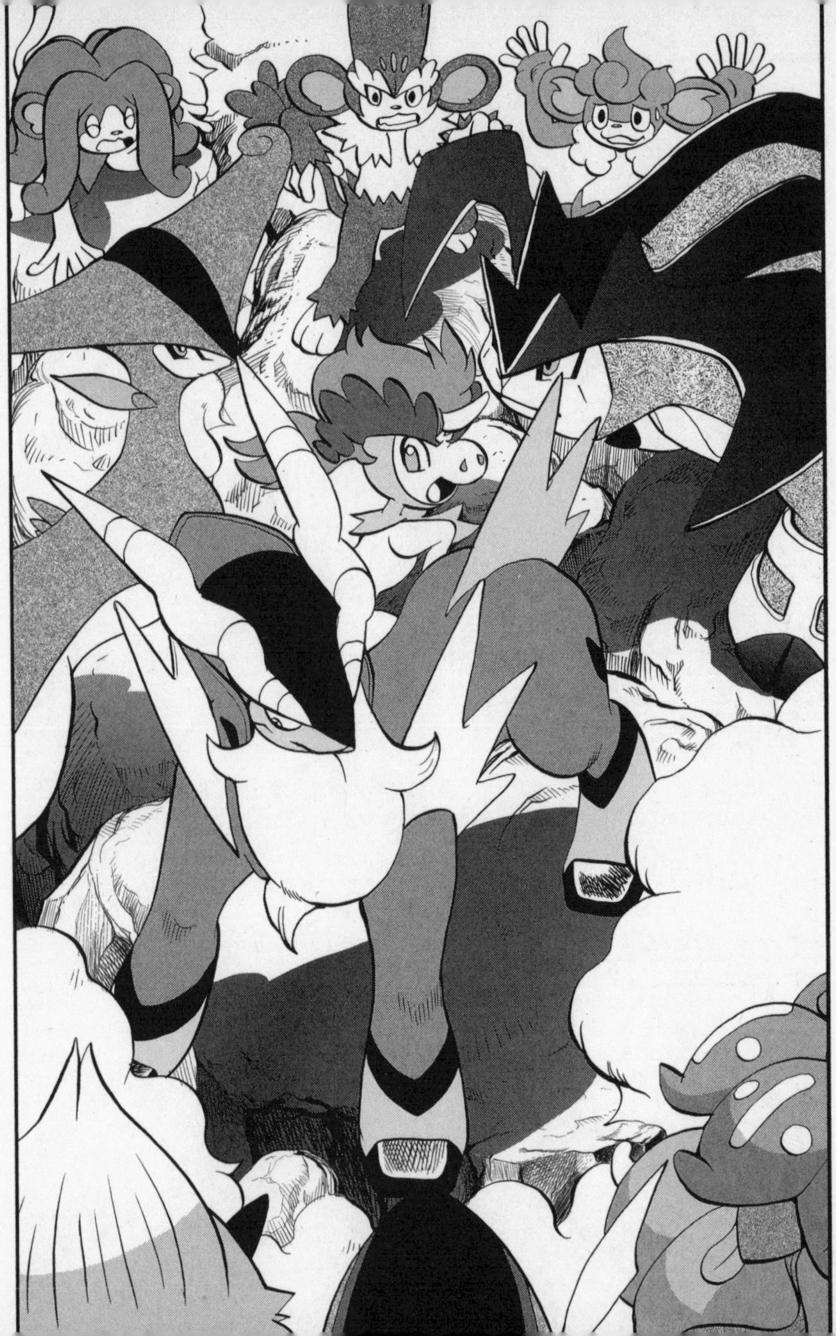

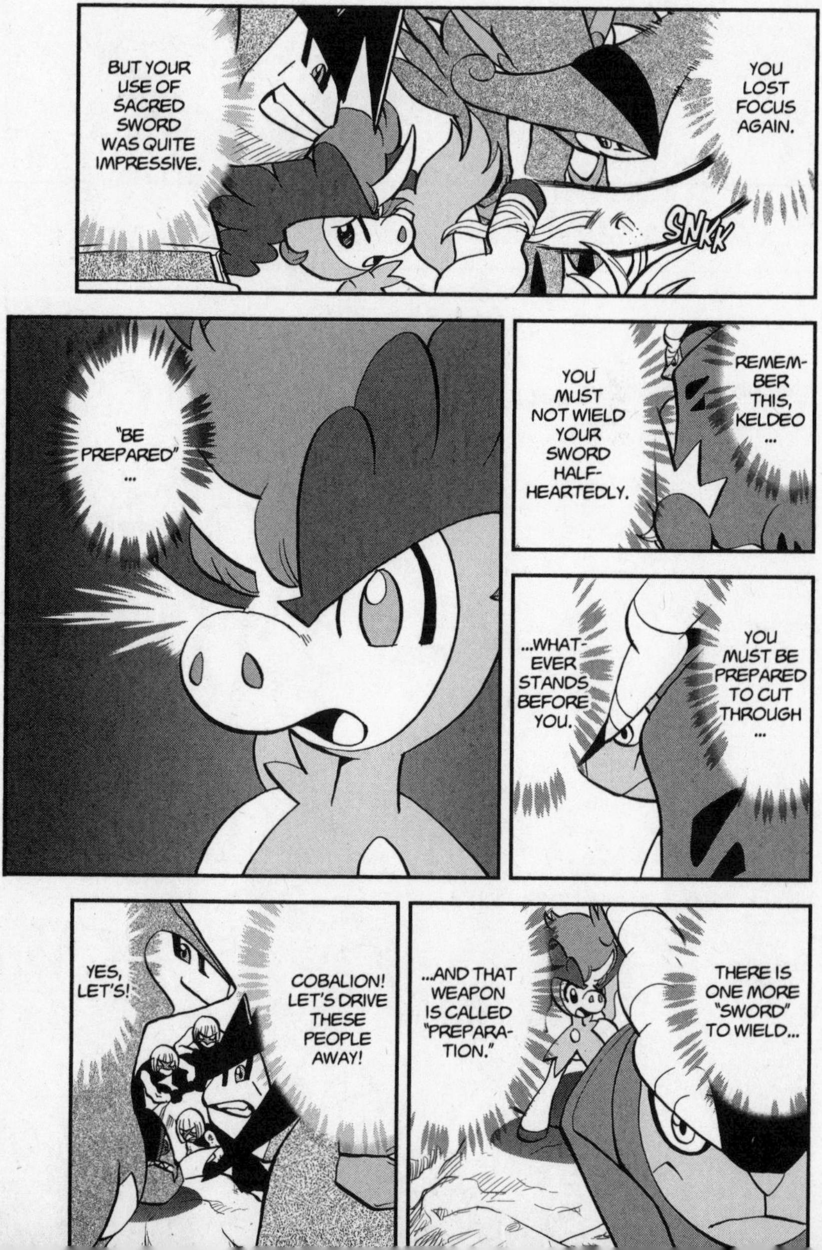
YOU LOST FOCUS AGAIN.
BUT YOUR USE OF SACRED SWORD WAS QUITE IMPRESSIVE.
SNKK
REMEMBER THIS, KELDEO ...
YOU MUST NOT WIELD YOUR SWORD HALF-HEARTEDLY.
YOU MUST BE PREPARED TO CUT THROUGH ...
...WHATEVER STANDS BEFORE YOU.
"BE PREPARED" ...
THERE IS ONE MORE "SWORD" TO WIELD...
...AND THAT WEAPON IS CALLED "PREPARATION."
COBALION! LET'S DRIVE THESE PEOPLE AWAY!
YES, LET'S!

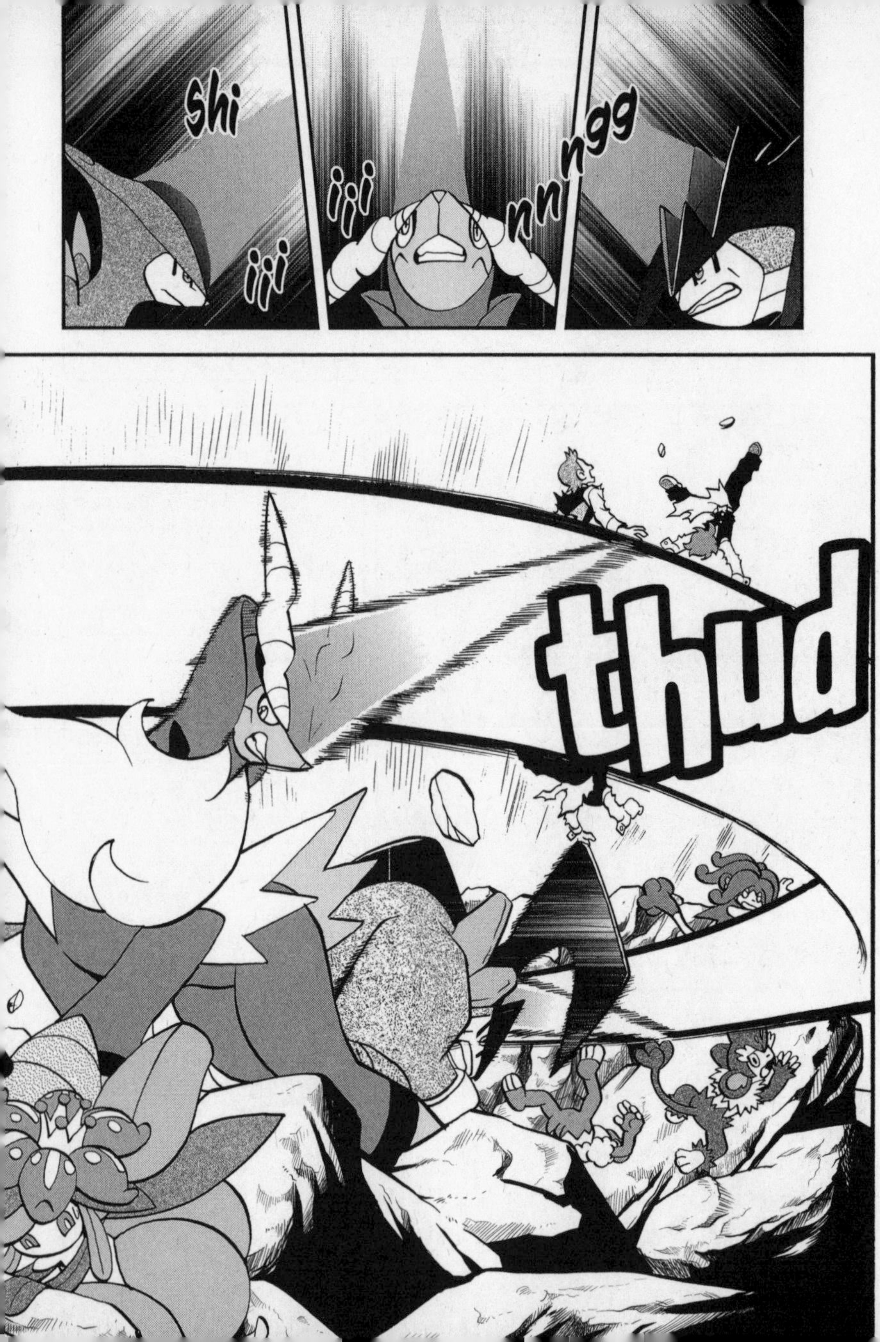
Shi
iii
iii
nnnngg
thud

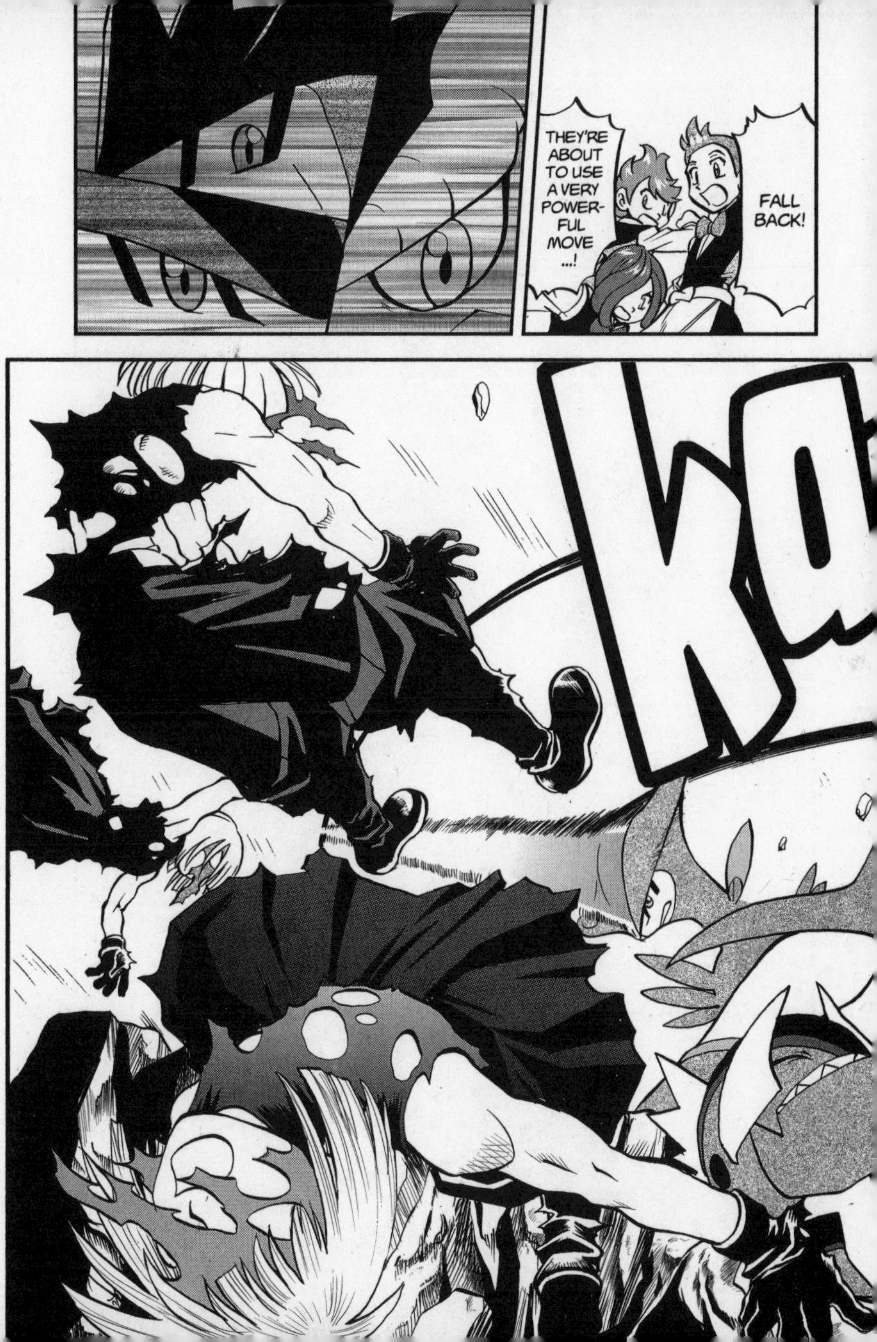
FALL BACK!
THEY'RE ABOUT TO USE A VERY POWERFUL MOVE ...!

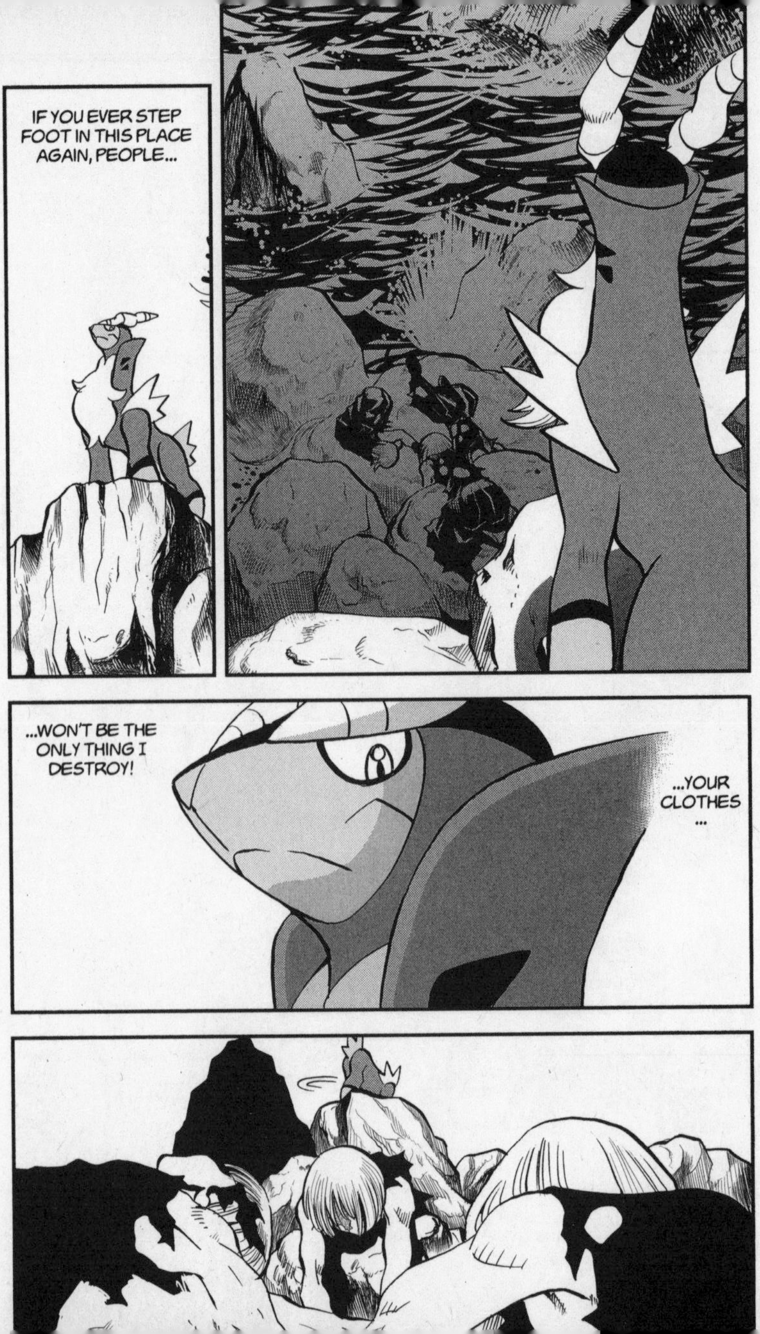
IF YOU EVER STEP FOOT IN THIS PLACE AGAIN, PEOPLE...
...WON'T BE THE ONLY THING I DESTROY!
...YOUR CLOTHES ...

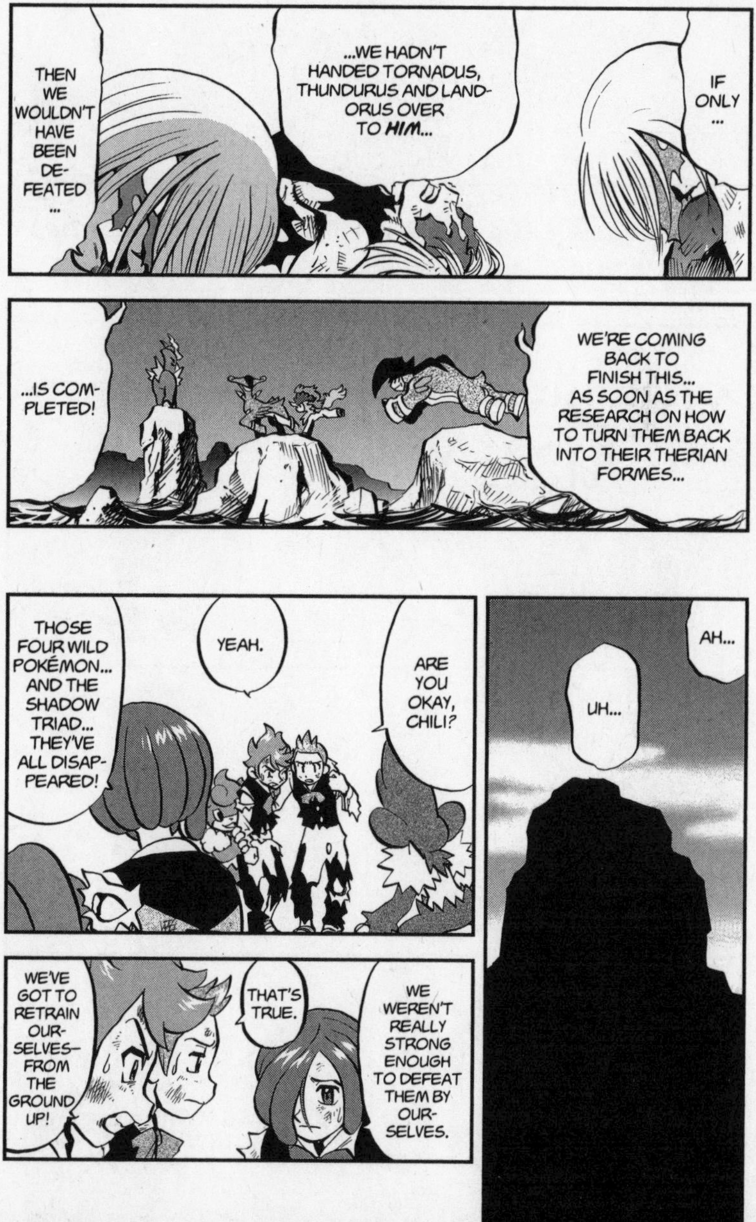
IF ONLY ...
...WE HADN'T HANDED TORNADUS, THUNDURUS AND LANDORUS OVER TO *HIM*...
THEN WE WOULDN'T HAVE BEEN DEFEATED ...
WE'RE COMING BACK TO FINISH THIS... AS SOON AS THE RESEARCH ON HOW TO TURN THEM BACK INTO THEIR THERIAN FORMES...
...IS COMPLETED!
AH...
UH...
ARE YOU OKAY, CHILI?
YEAH.
THOSE FOUR WILD POKÉMON... AND THE SHADOW TRIAD... THEY'VE ALL DISAPPEARED!
WE WEREN'T REALLY STRONG ENOUGH TO DEFEAT THEM BY OURSELVES.
THAT'S TRUE.
WE'VE GOT TO RETRAIN OURSELVES—FROM THE GROUND UP!

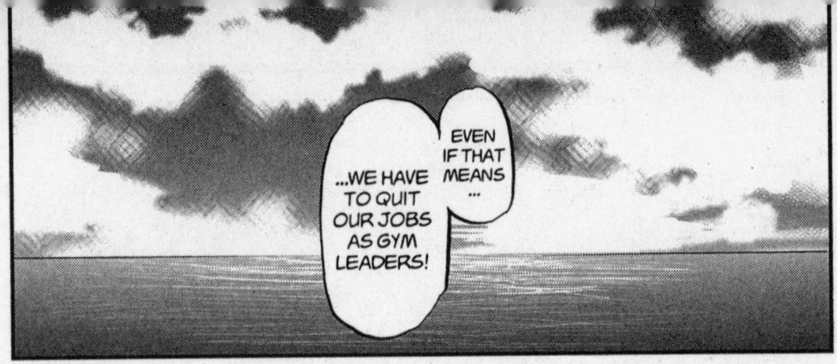
EVEN IF THAT MEANS ...
...WE HAVE TO QUIT OUR JOBS AS GYM LEADERS!

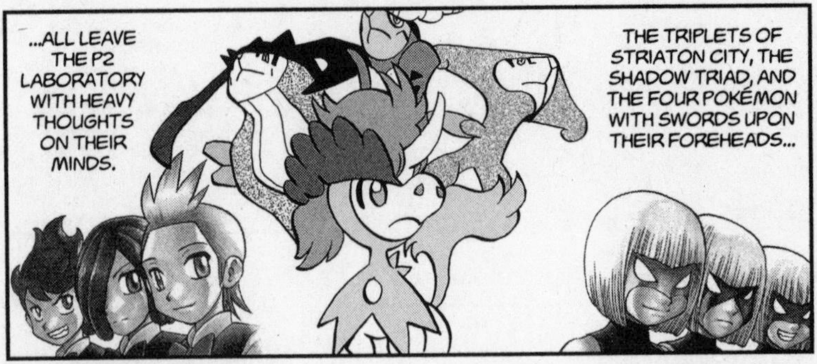
THE TRIPLETS OF STRIATON CITY, THE SHADOW TRIAD, AND THE FOUR POKÉMON WITH SWORDS UPON THEIR FOREHEADS...
...ALL LEAVE THE P2 LABORATORY WITH HEAVY THOUGHTS ON THEIR MINDS.

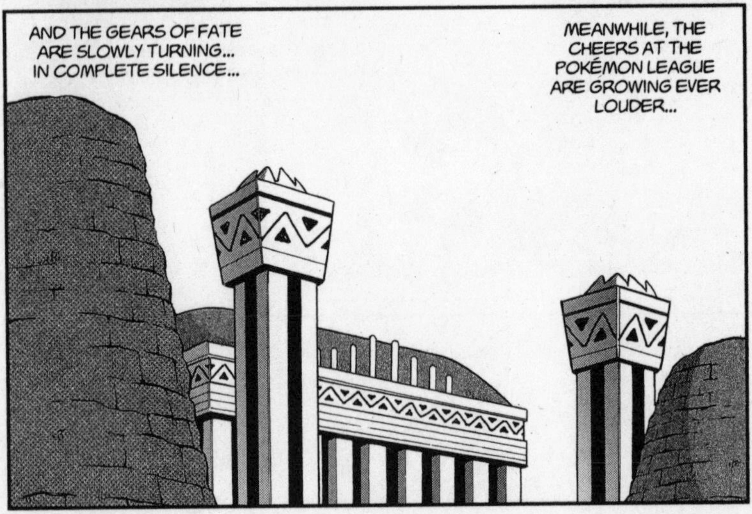
MEANWHILE, THE CHEERS AT THE POKÉMON LEAGUE ARE GROWING EVER LOUDER...
AND THE GEARS OF FATE ARE SLOWLY TURNING... IN COMPLETE SILENCE...

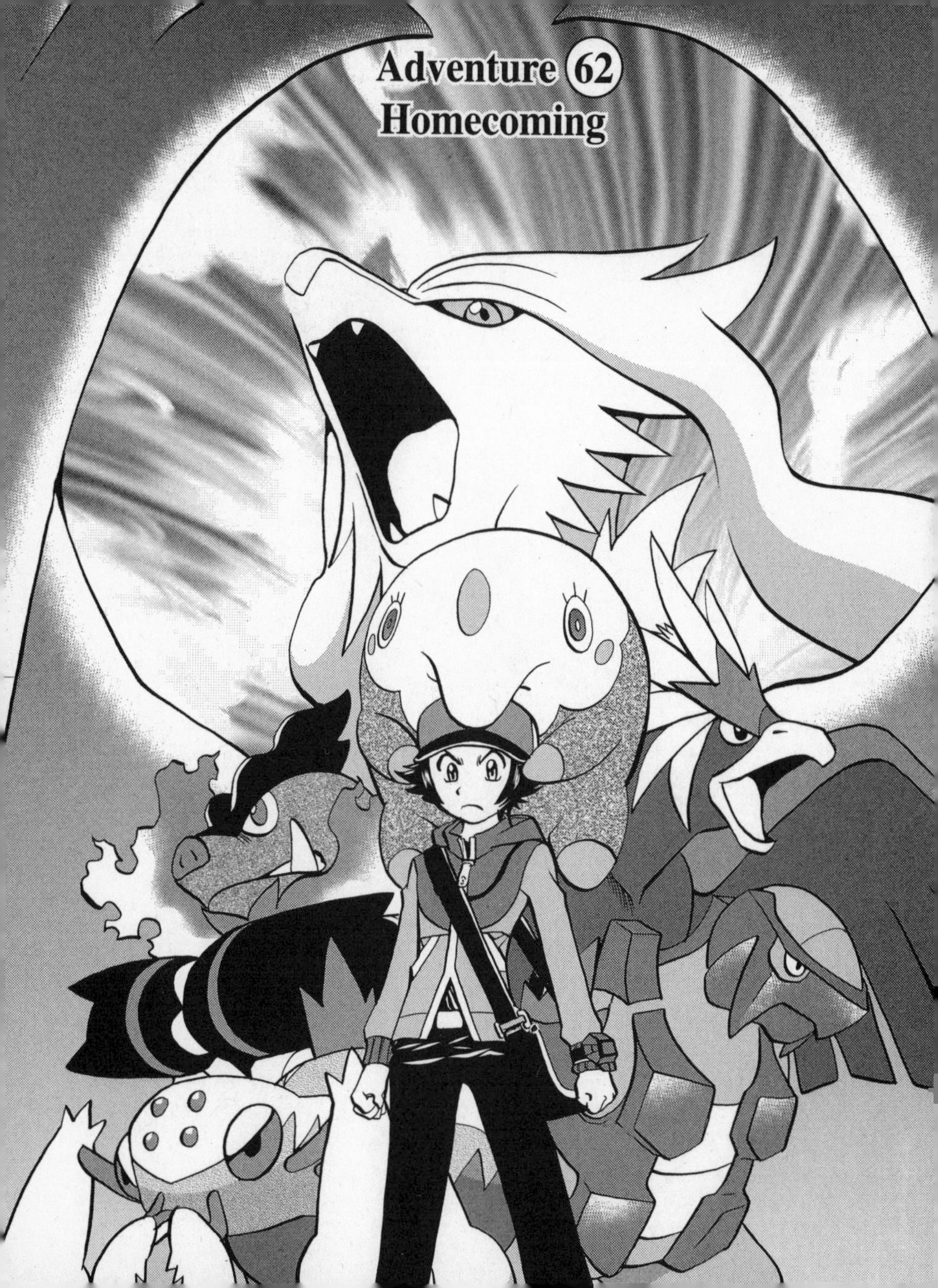
Adventure 62
Homecoming

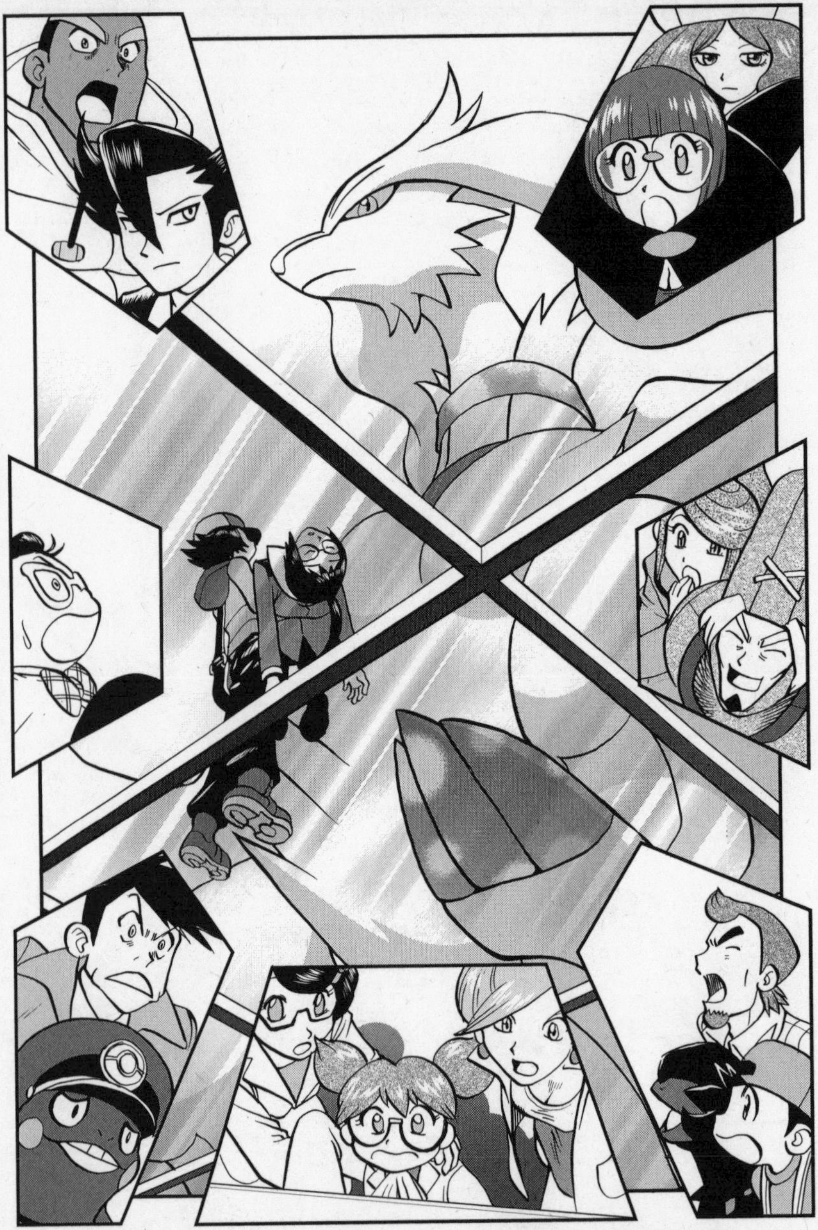

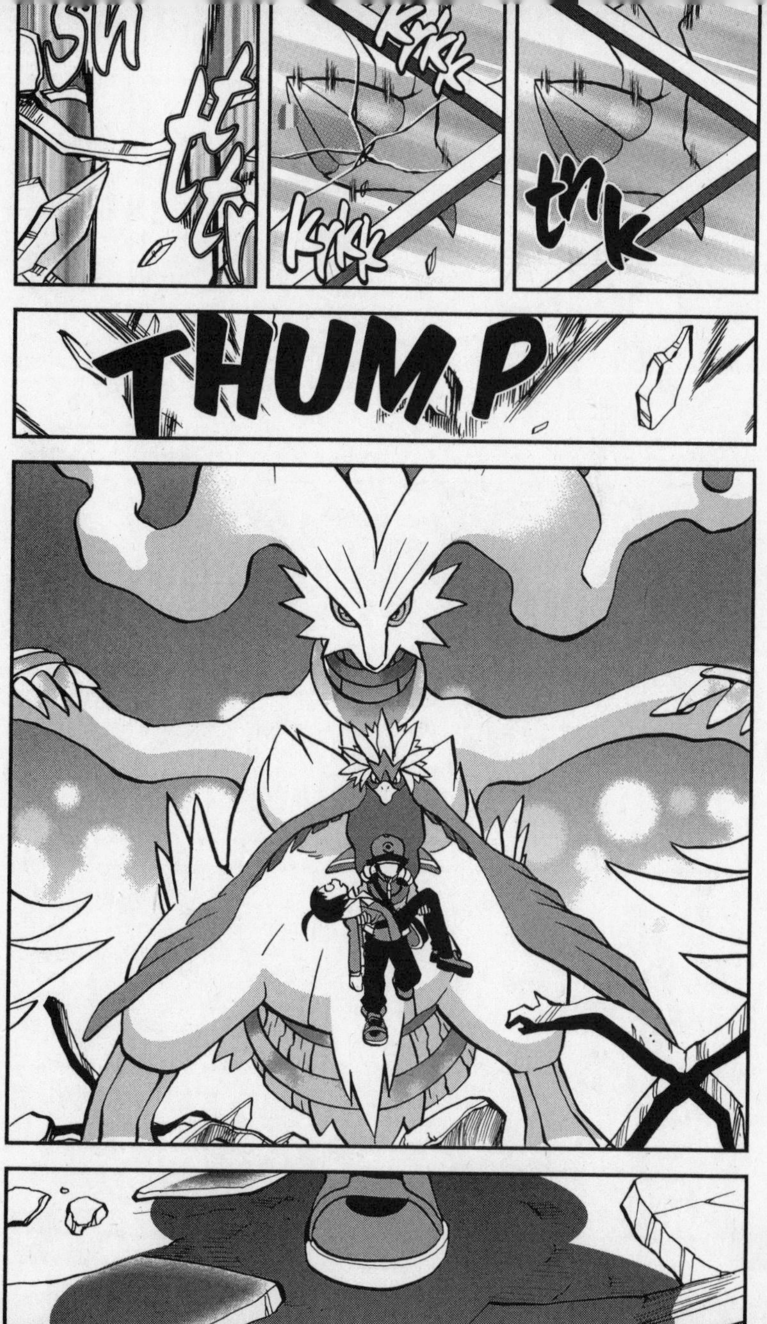
tink
Krikk
Krikk
THUMP

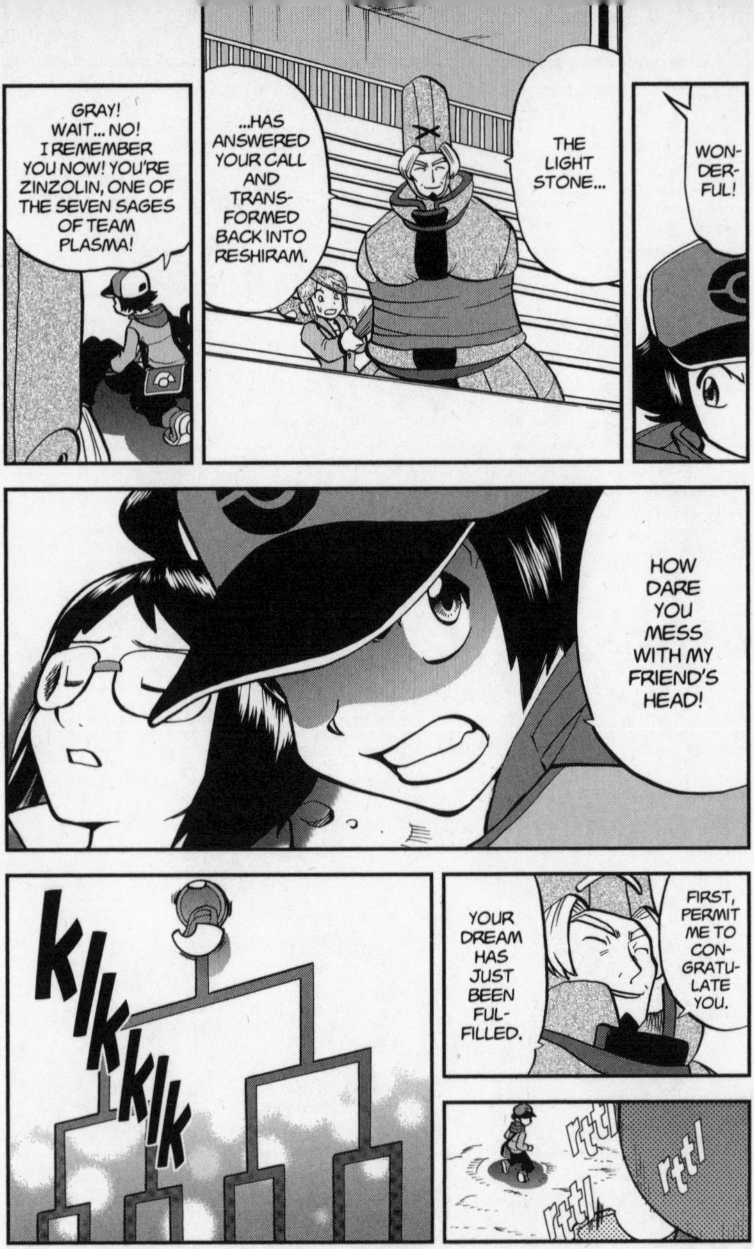
WONDERFUL!
THE LIGHT STONE...
...HAS ANSWERED YOUR CALL AND TRANSFORMED BACK INTO RESHIRAM.
GRAY! WAIT... NO! I REMEMBER YOU NOW! YOU'RE ZINZOLIN, ONE OF THE SEVEN SAGES OF TEAM PLASMA!
HOW DARE YOU MESS WITH MY FRIEND'S HEAD!
FIRST, PERMIT ME TO CONGRATULATE YOU.
YOUR DREAM HAS JUST BEEN FULFILLED.
rttl
rttl
rttl
rttl
KIKKKIK

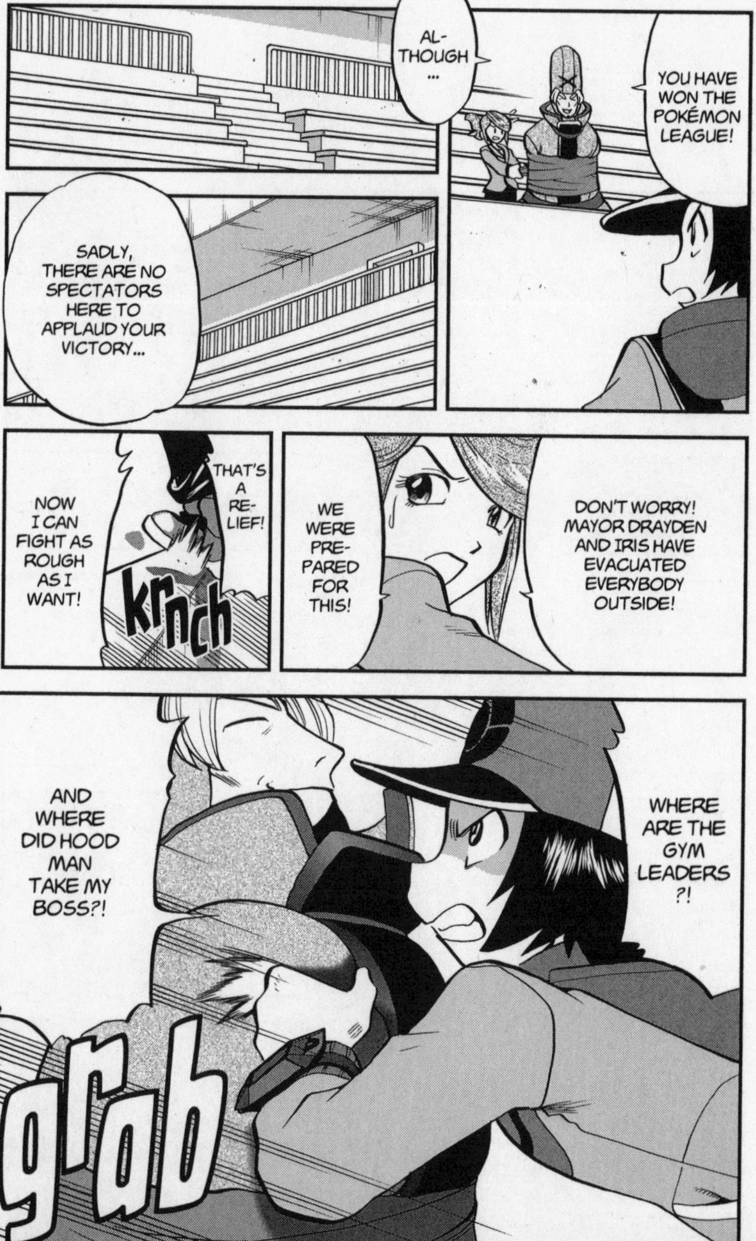
YOU HAVE WON THE POKÉMON LEAGUE!
AL-THOUGH...
SADLY, THERE ARE NO SPECTATORS HERE TO APPLAUD YOUR VICTORY...
DON'T WORRY! MAYOR DRAYDEN AND IRIS HAVE EVACUATED EVERYBODY OUTSIDE!
WE WERE PRE-PARED FOR THIS!
THAT'S A RE-LIEF!
NOW I CAN FIGHT AS ROUGH AS I WANT!
krnch
WHERE ARE THE GYM LEADERS ?!
AND WHERE DID HOOD MAN TAKE MY BOSS?!
grab

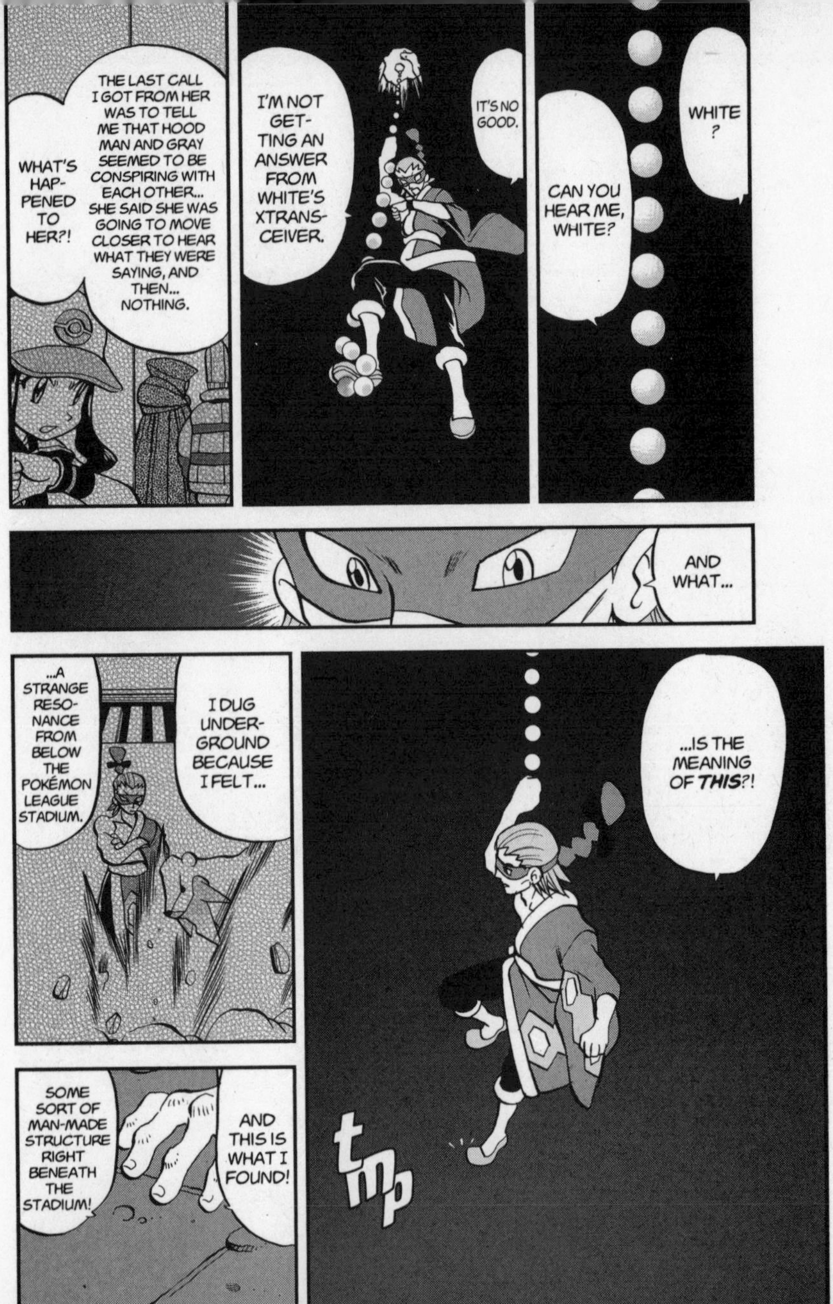
WHITE?
CAN YOU HEAR ME, WHITE?
IT'S NO GOOD.
I'M NOT GETTING AN ANSWER FROM WHITE'S XTRANSCEIVER.
THE LAST CALL I GOT FROM HER WAS TO TELL ME THAT HOOD MAN AND GRAY SEEMED TO BE CONSPIRING WITH EACH OTHER... SHE SAID SHE WAS GOING TO MOVE CLOSER TO HEAR WHAT THEY WERE SAYING, AND THEN... NOTHING.
WHAT'S HAPPENED TO HER?!
AND WHAT...
...IS THE MEANING OF THIS?!
tmp
I DUG UNDERGROUND BECAUSE I FELT...
...A STRANGE RESONANCE FROM BELOW THE POKÉMON LEAGUE STADIUM.
AND THIS IS WHAT I FOUND!
SOME SORT OF MAN-MADE STRUCTURE RIGHT BENEATH THE STADIUM!

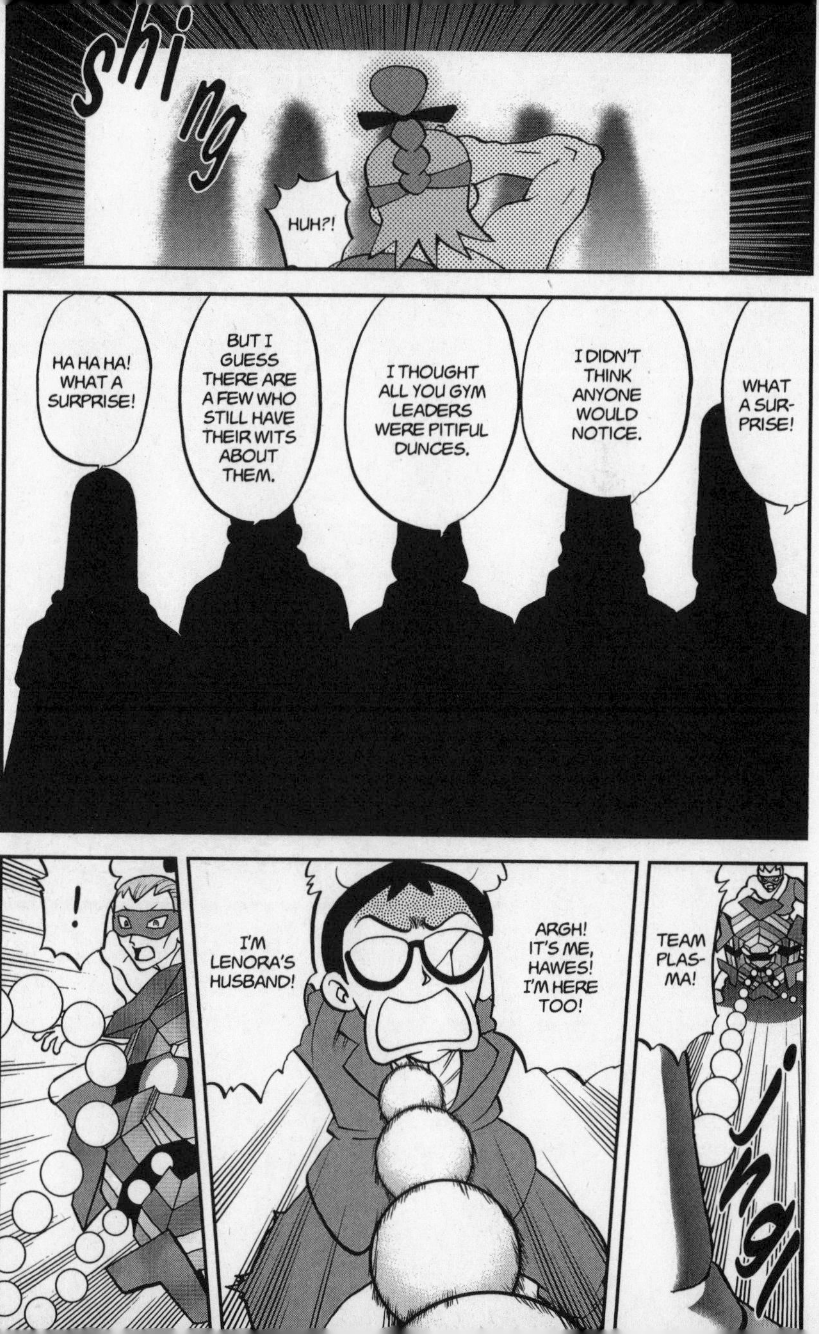
shi ng
HUH?!
WHAT A SURPRISE!
I DIDN'T THINK ANYONE WOULD NOTICE.
I THOUGHT ALL YOU GYM LEADERS WERE PITIFUL DUNCES.
BUT I GUESS THERE ARE A FEW WHO STILL HAVE THEIR WITS ABOUT THEM.
HA HA HA! WHAT A SURPRISE!
TEAM PLASMA!
jingl
ARGH! IT'S ME, HAWES! I'M HERE TOO!
I'M LENORA'S HUSBAND!
!

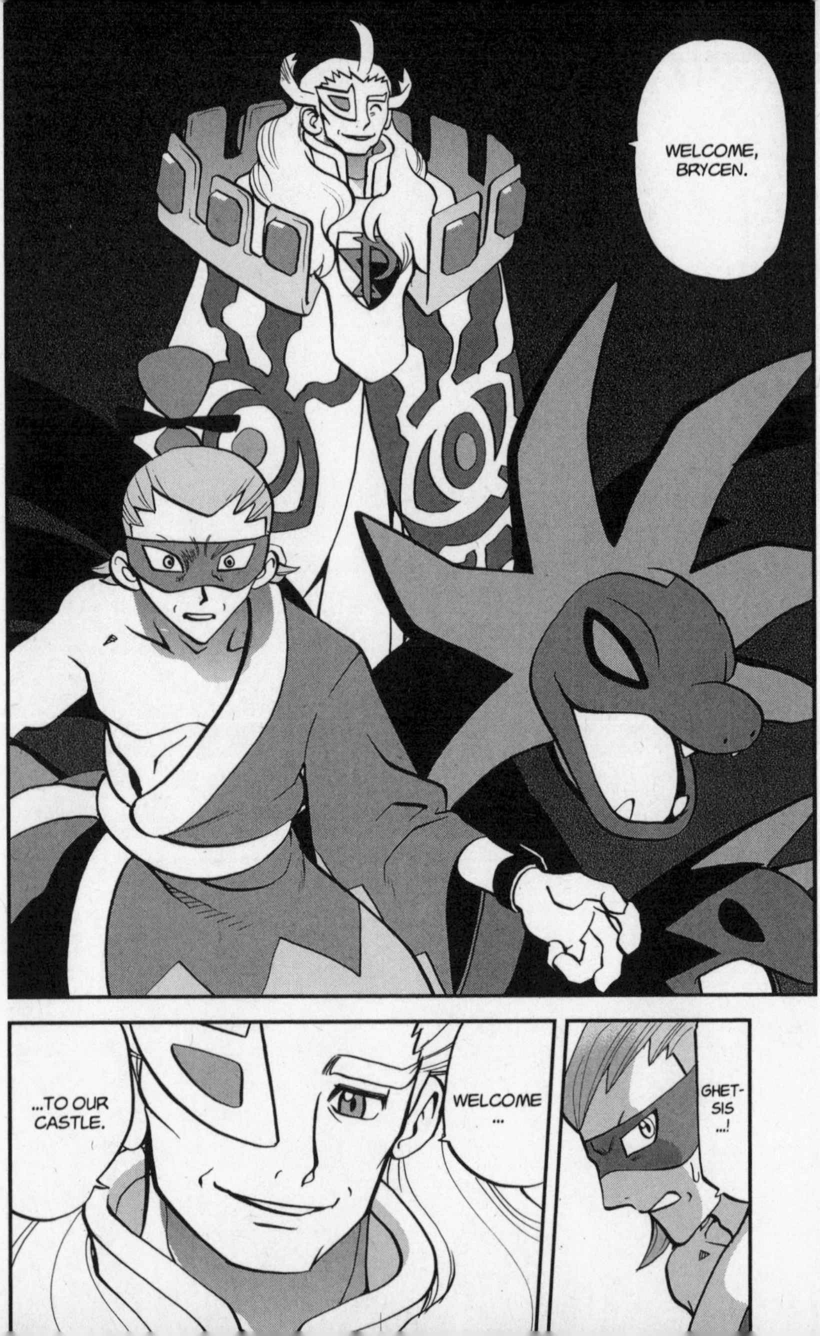
WELCOME, BRYCEN.
GHET-SIS ...!
WELCOME ...
...TO OUR CASTLE.

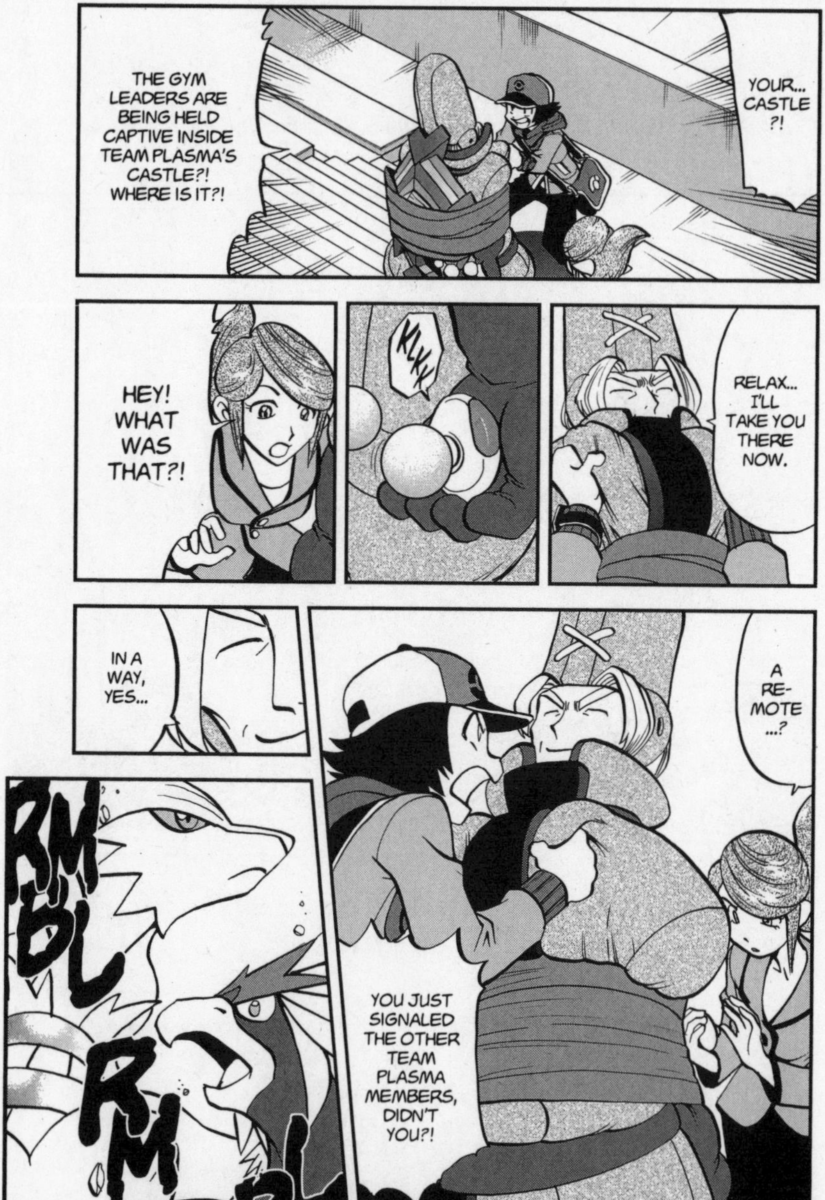
YOUR... CASTLE?!
THE GYM LEADERS ARE BEING HELD CAPTIVE INSIDE TEAM PLASMA'S CASTLE?! WHERE IS IT?!
RELAX... I'LL TAKE YOU THERE NOW.
KLKK
HEY! WHAT WAS THAT?!
A RE-MOTE...?
YOU JUST SIGNALED THE OTHER TEAM PLASMA MEMBERS, DIDN'T YOU?!
IN A WAY, YES...
RMBL
RMBL

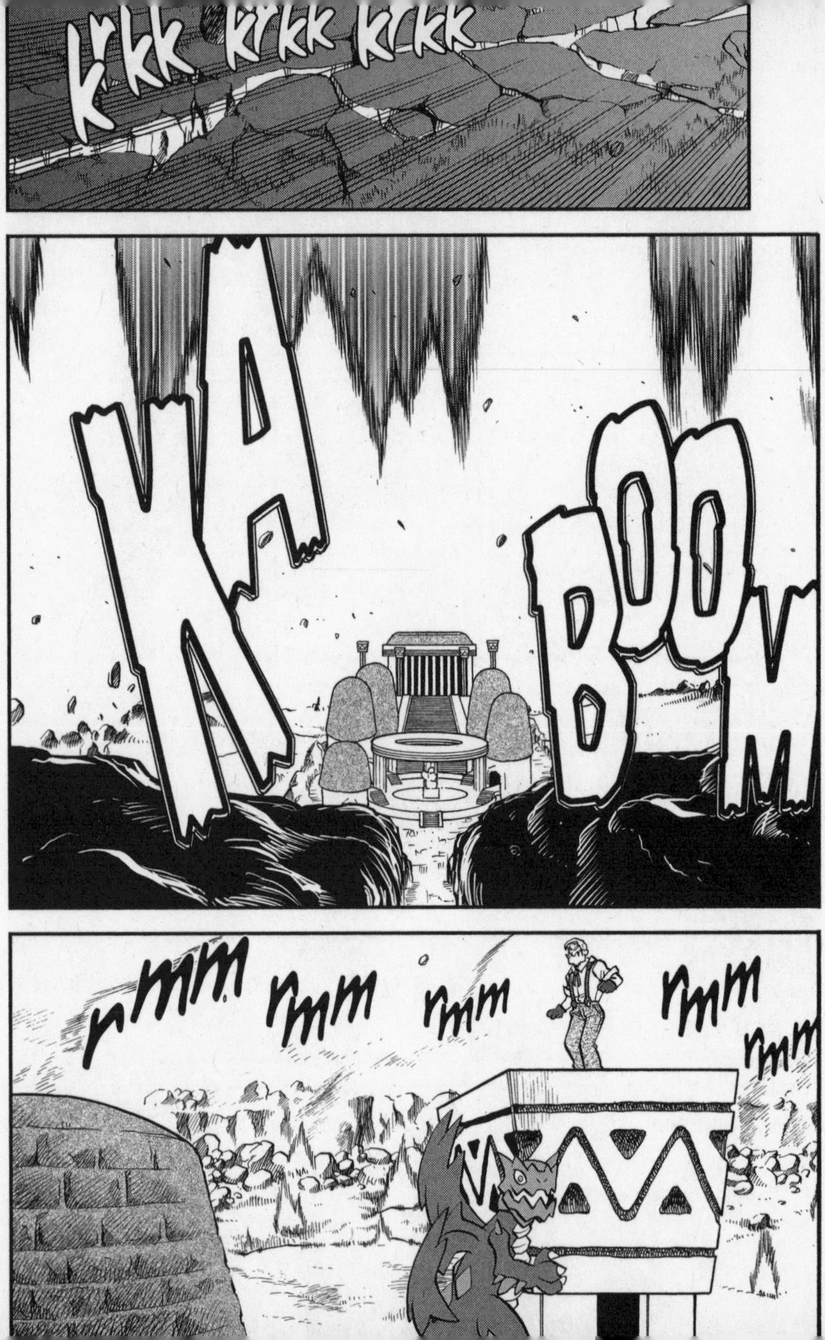
krkk krkk krkk
KA
BOOM
rmm rmm rmm rmm rmm

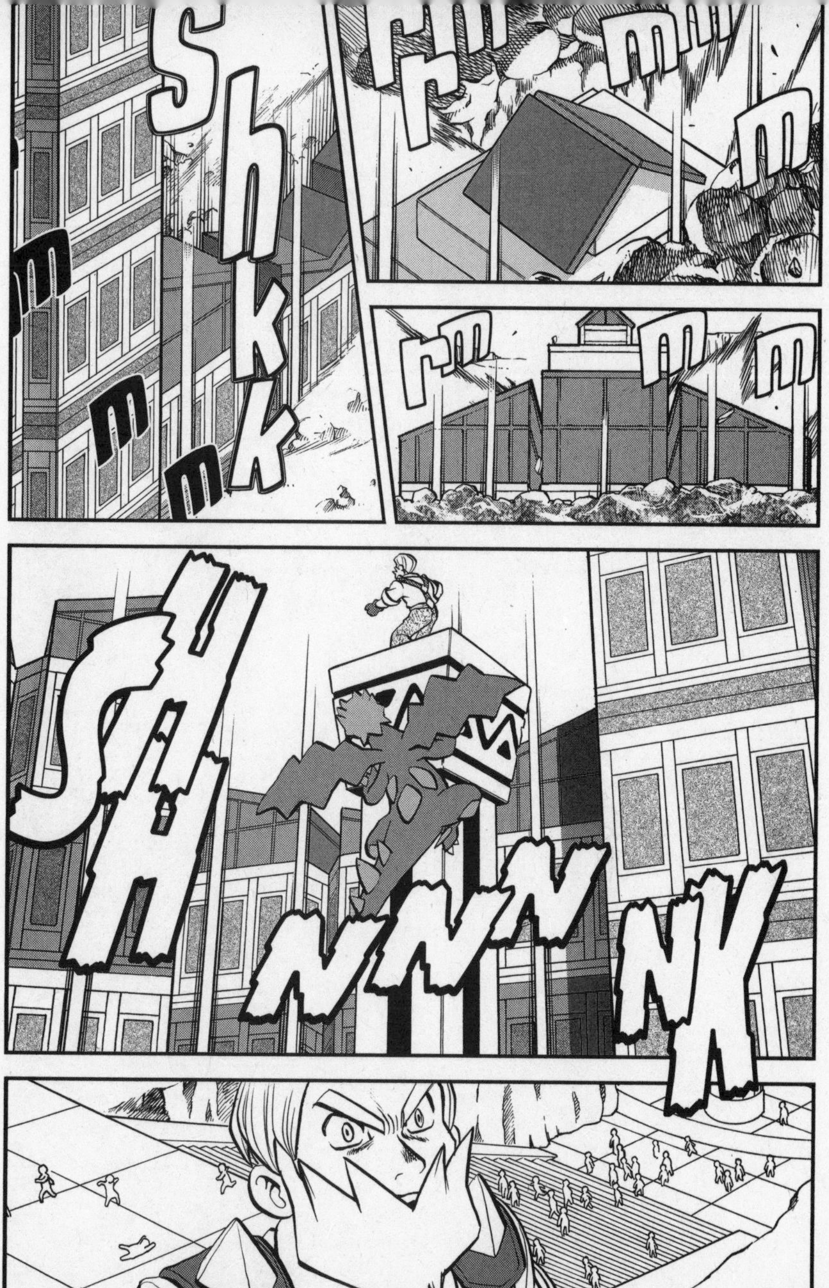
rrmmmm
rmmm
Shkk
mmm
SHNNNK

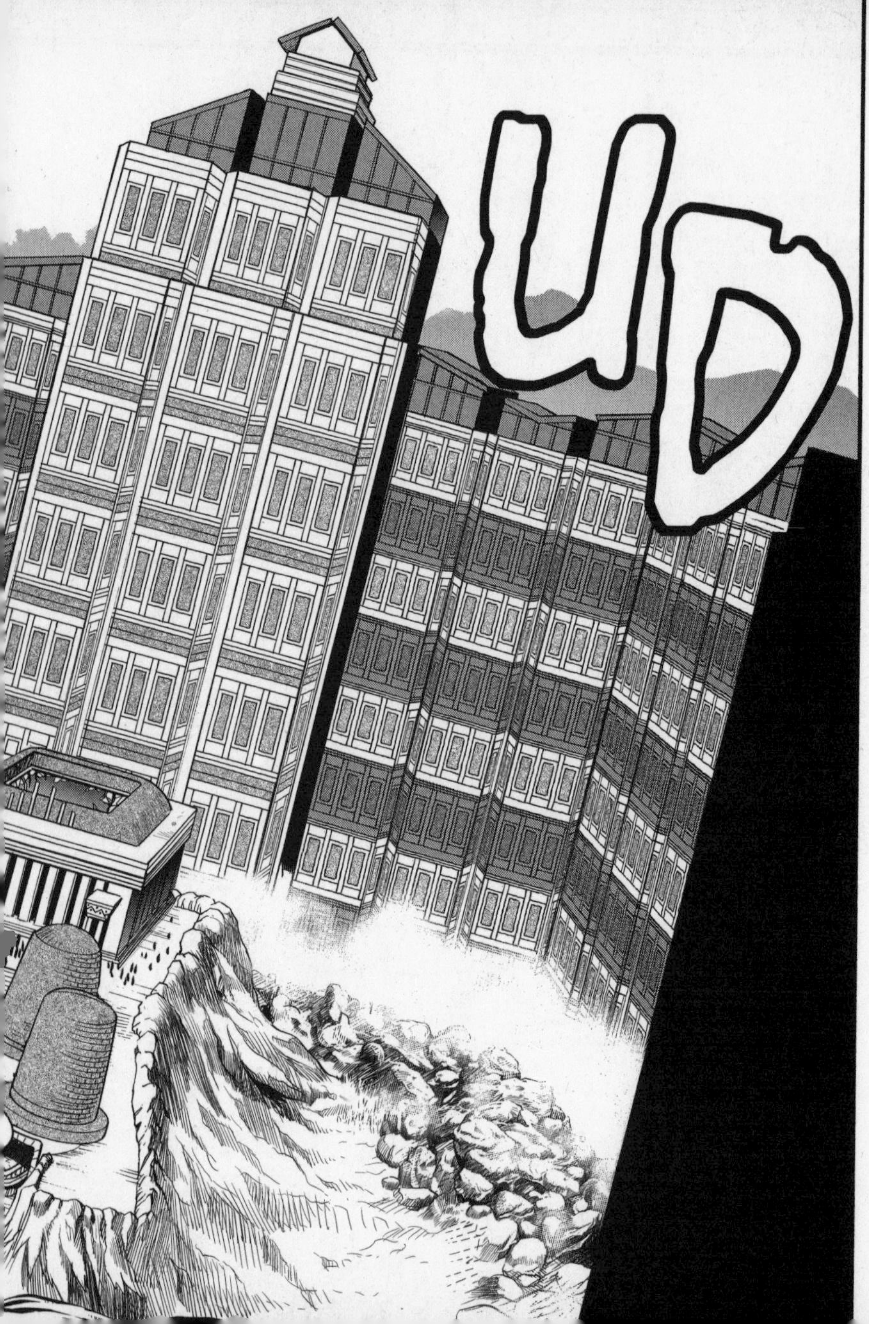
UD

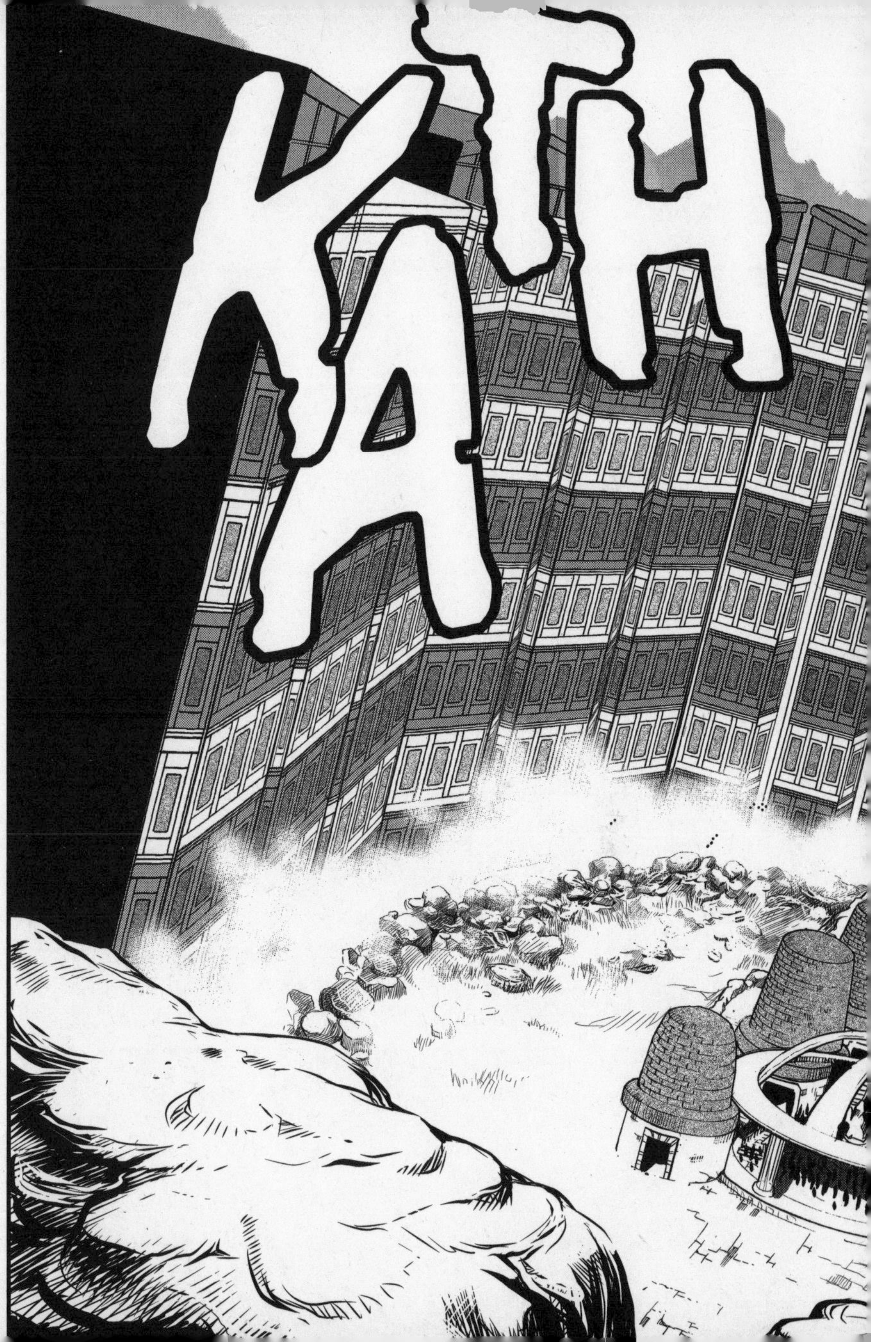
KATH

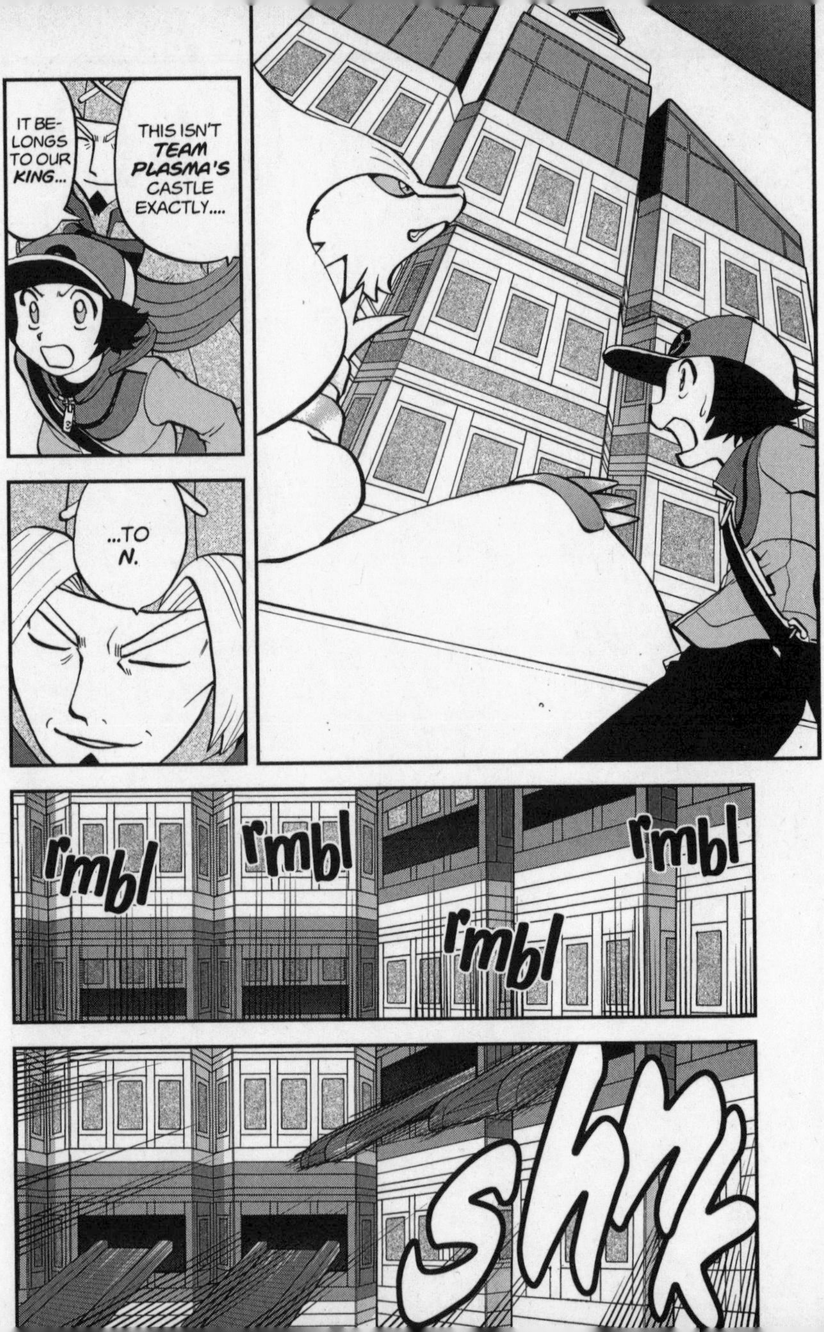
THIS ISN'T TEAM PLASMA'S CASTLE EXACTLY....
IT BE-LONGS TO OUR KING...
...TO N.
rmbl
rmbl
rmbl
rmbl
shk

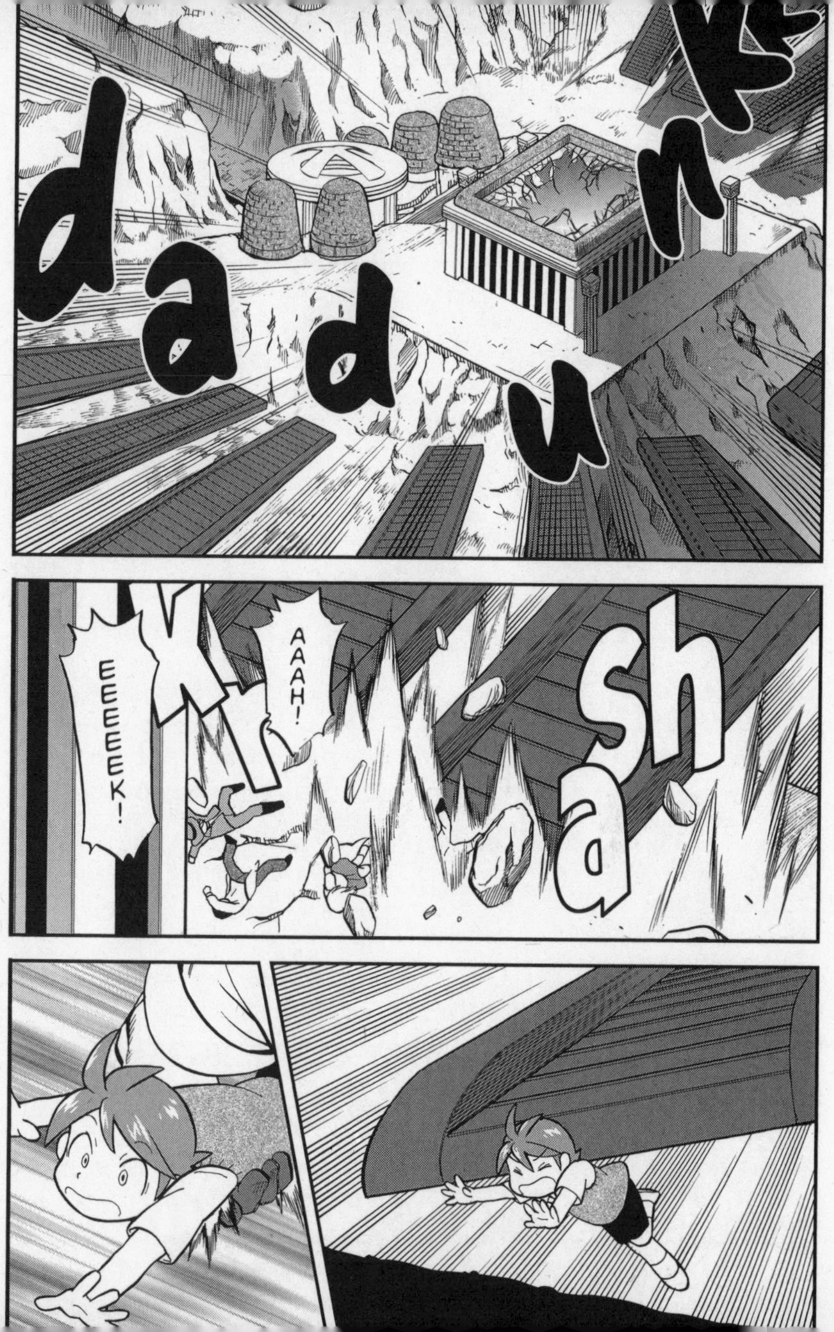
dadunk
AAAH!
EEEEEEK!

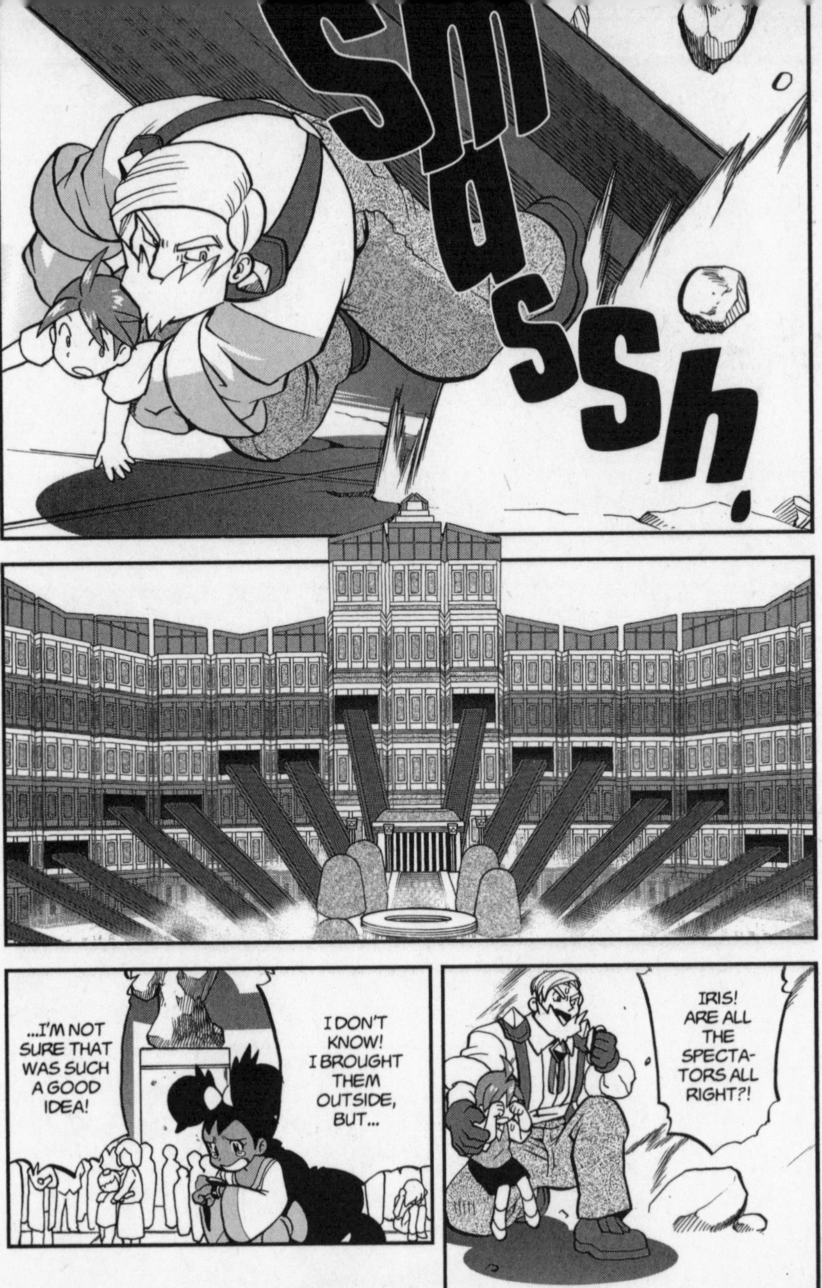
SMASSH!
IRIS! ARE ALL THE SPECTATORS ALL RIGHT?!
I DON'T KNOW! I BROUGHT THEM OUTSIDE, BUT...
...I'M NOT SURE THAT WAS SUCH A GOOD IDEA!

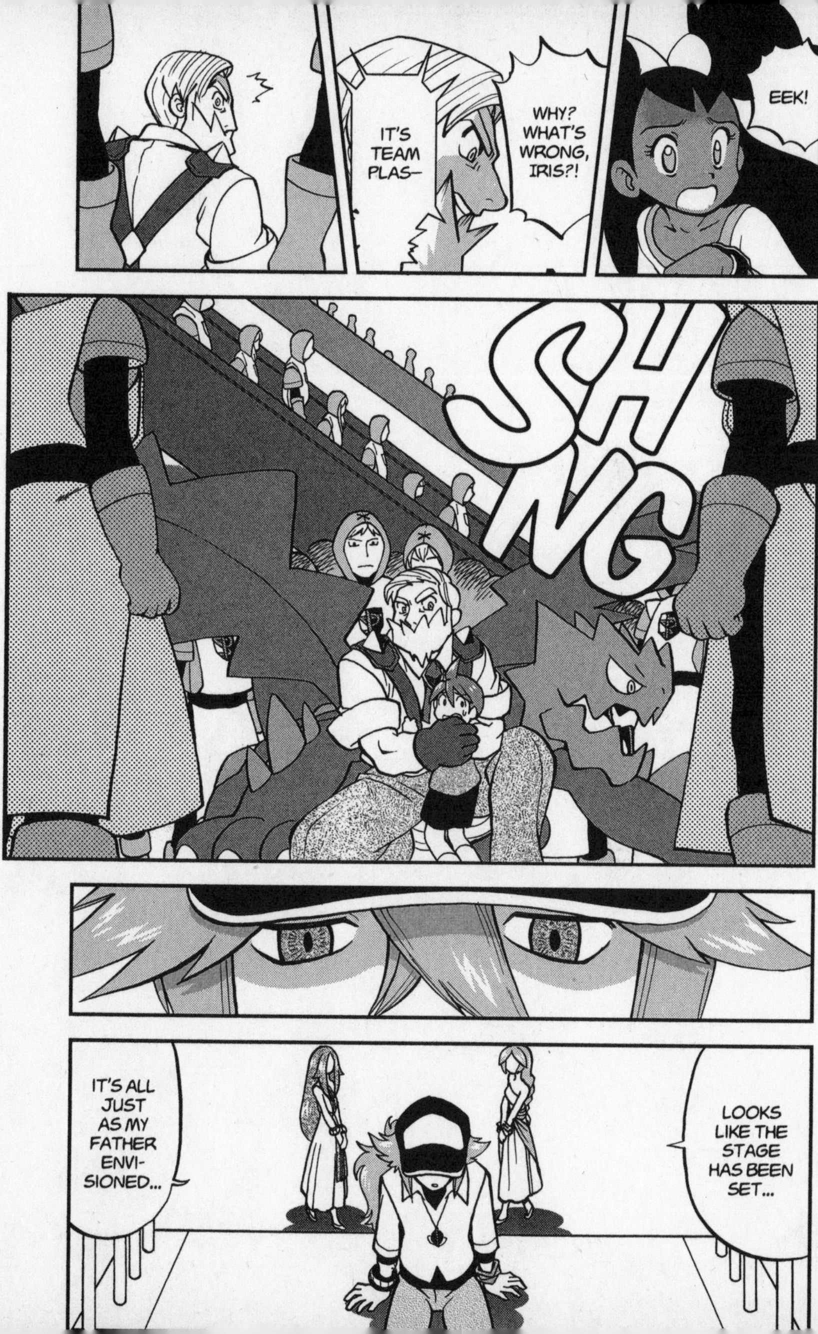
EEK!
WHY? WHAT'S WRONG, IRIS?!
IT'S TEAM PLAS–
SHING
LOOKS LIKE THE STAGE HAS BEEN SET...
IT'S ALL JUST AS MY FATHER ENVISIONED...

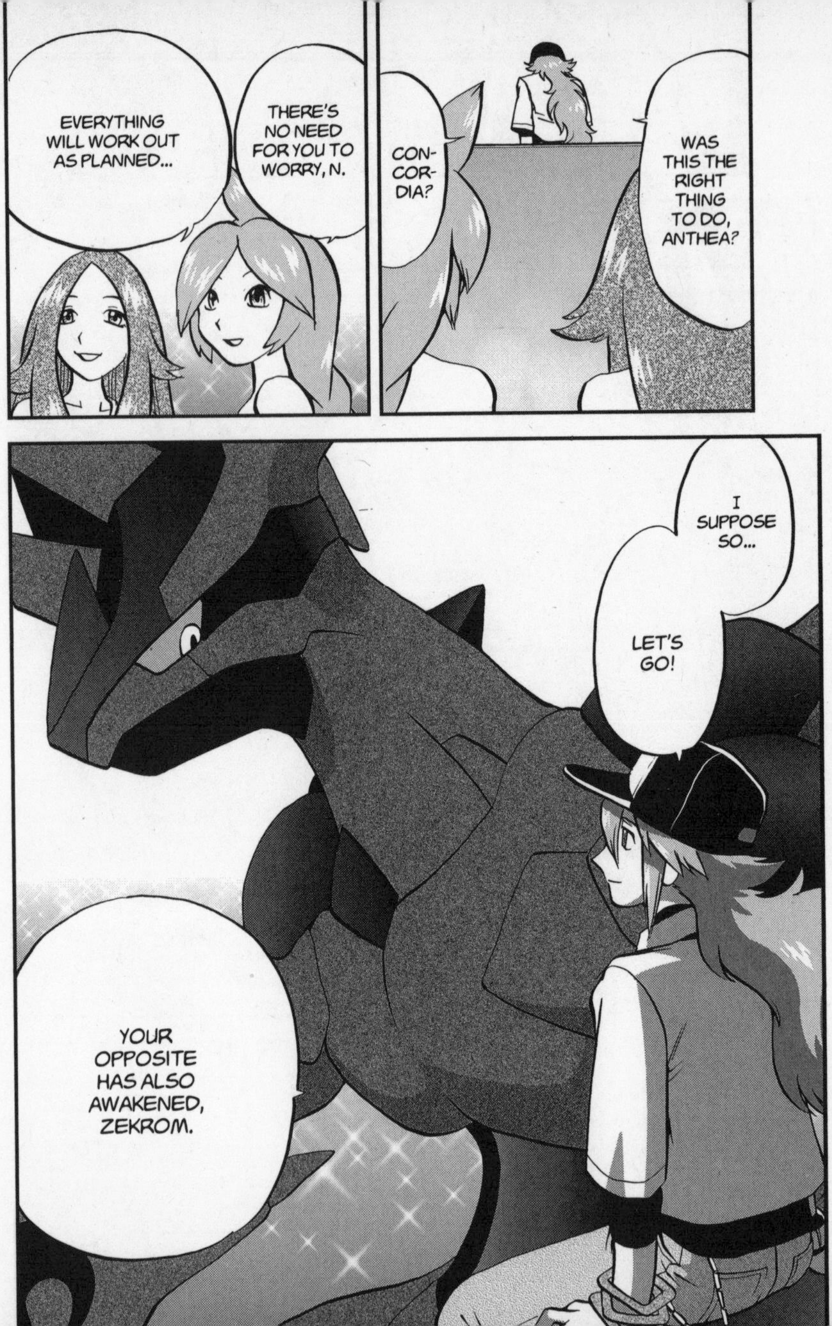
WAS THIS THE RIGHT THING TO DO, ANTHEA?
CON-COR-DIA?
THERE'S NO NEED FOR YOU TO WORRY, N.
EVERYTHING WILL WORK OUT AS PLANNED...
I SUPPOSE SO...
LET'S GO!
YOUR OPPOSITE HAS ALSO AWAKENED, ZEKROM.

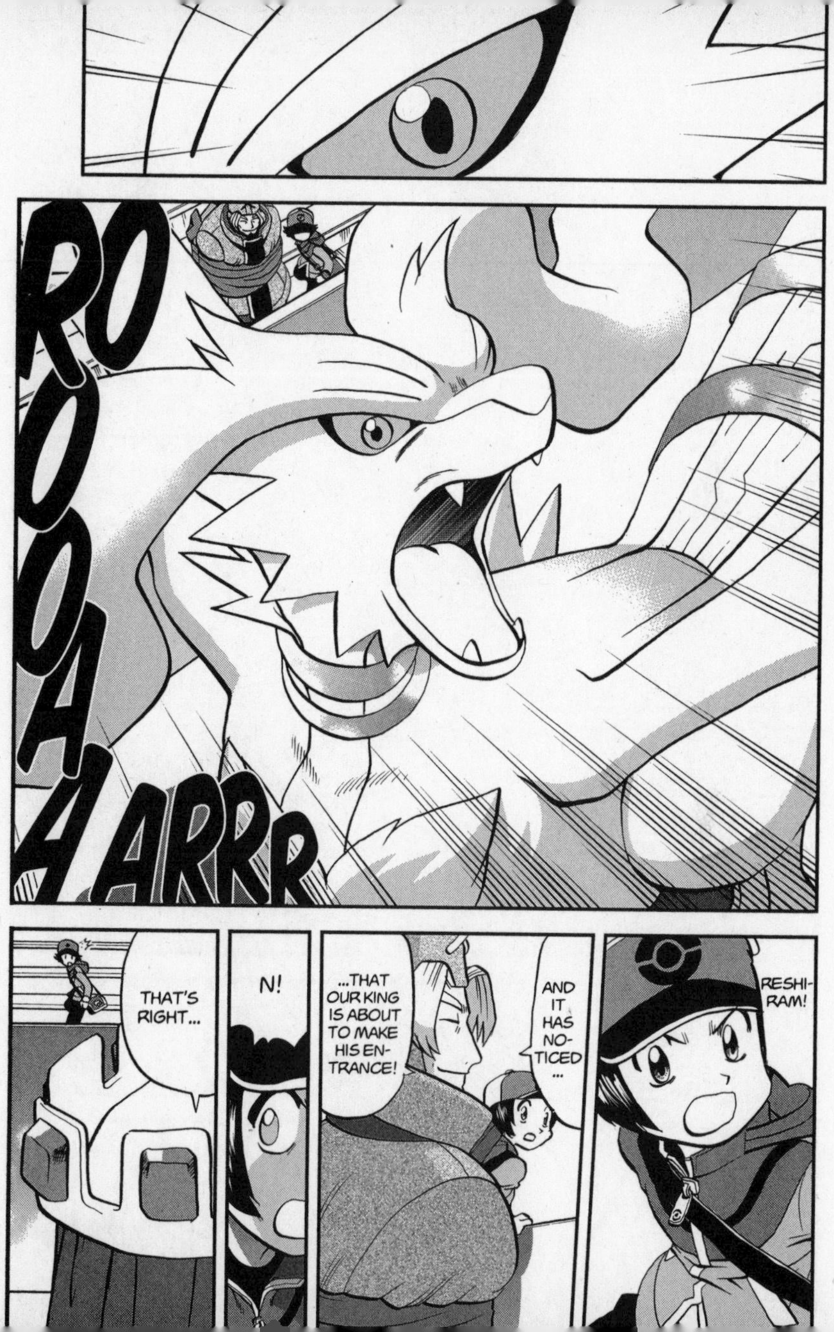
ROOOAAARRR
RESHIRAM!
AND IT HAS NOTICED...
...THAT OUR KING IS ABOUT TO MAKE HIS ENTRANCE!
N!
THAT'S RIGHT...

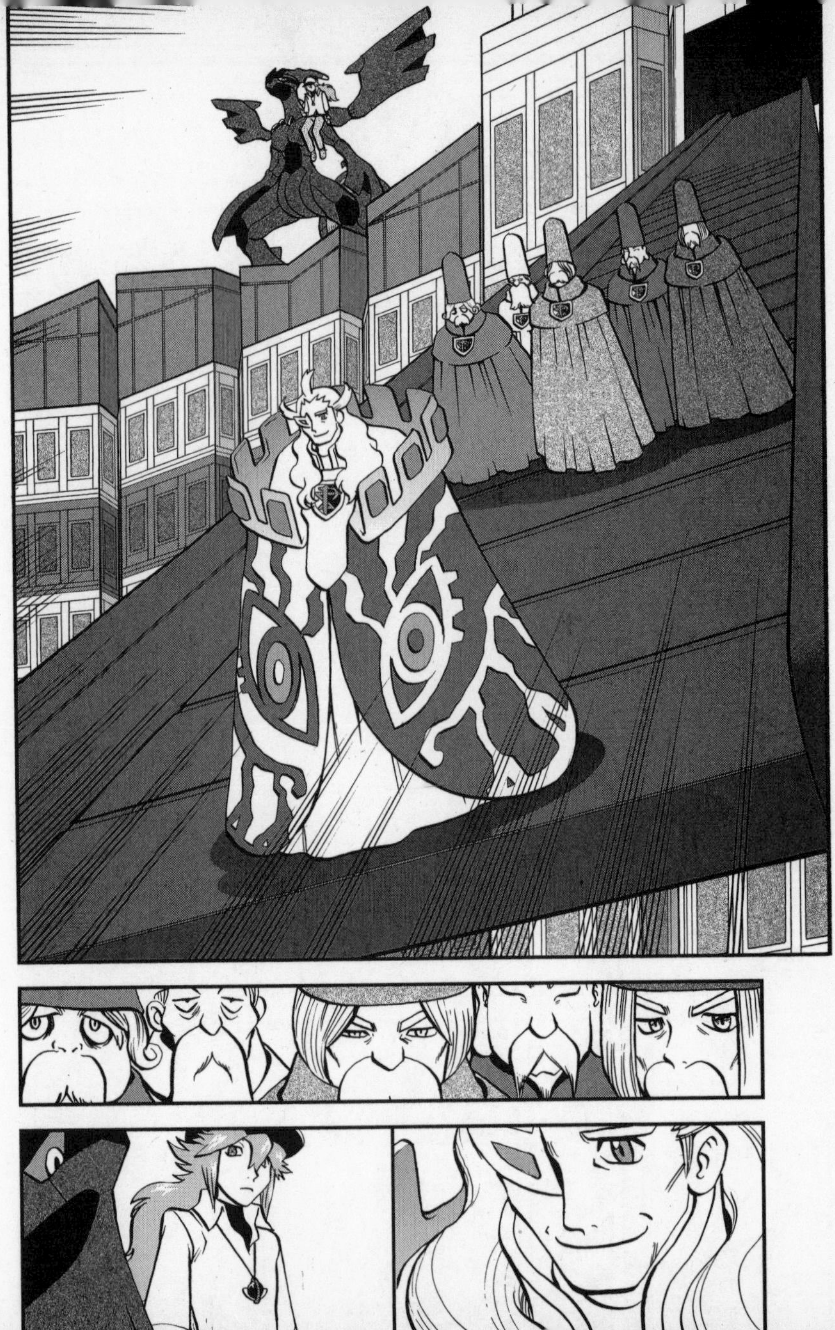

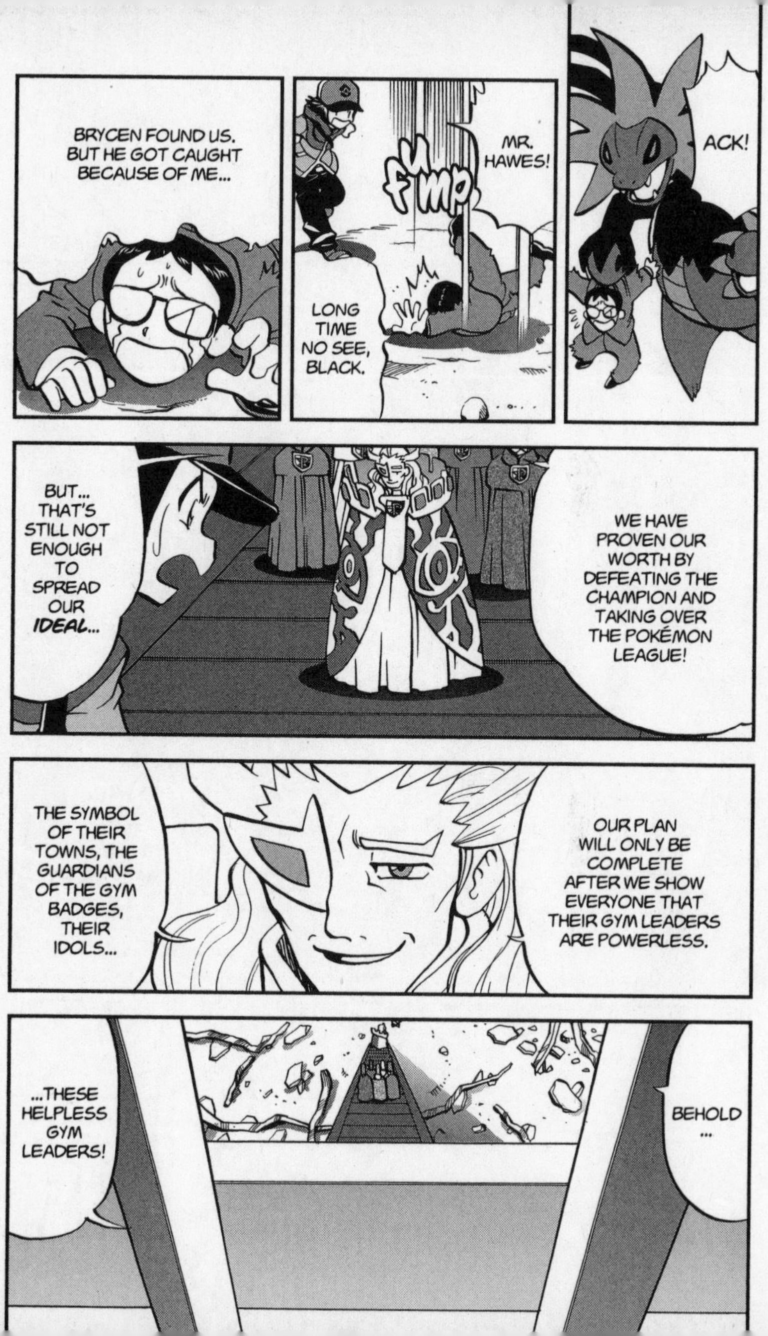
ACK!
MR. HAWES!
FUMP
LONG TIME NO SEE, BLACK.
BRYCEN FOUND US. BUT HE GOT CAUGHT BECAUSE OF ME...
WE HAVE PROVEN OUR WORTH BY DEFEATING THE CHAMPION AND TAKING OVER THE POKÉMON LEAGUE!
BUT... THAT'S STILL NOT ENOUGH TO SPREAD OUR *IDEAL*...
OUR PLAN WILL ONLY BE COMPLETE AFTER WE SHOW EVERYONE THAT THEIR GYM LEADERS ARE POWERLESS.
THE SYMBOL OF THEIR TOWNS, THE GUARDIANS OF THE GYM BADGES, THEIR IDOLS...
BEHOLD...
...THESE HELPLESS GYM LEADERS!

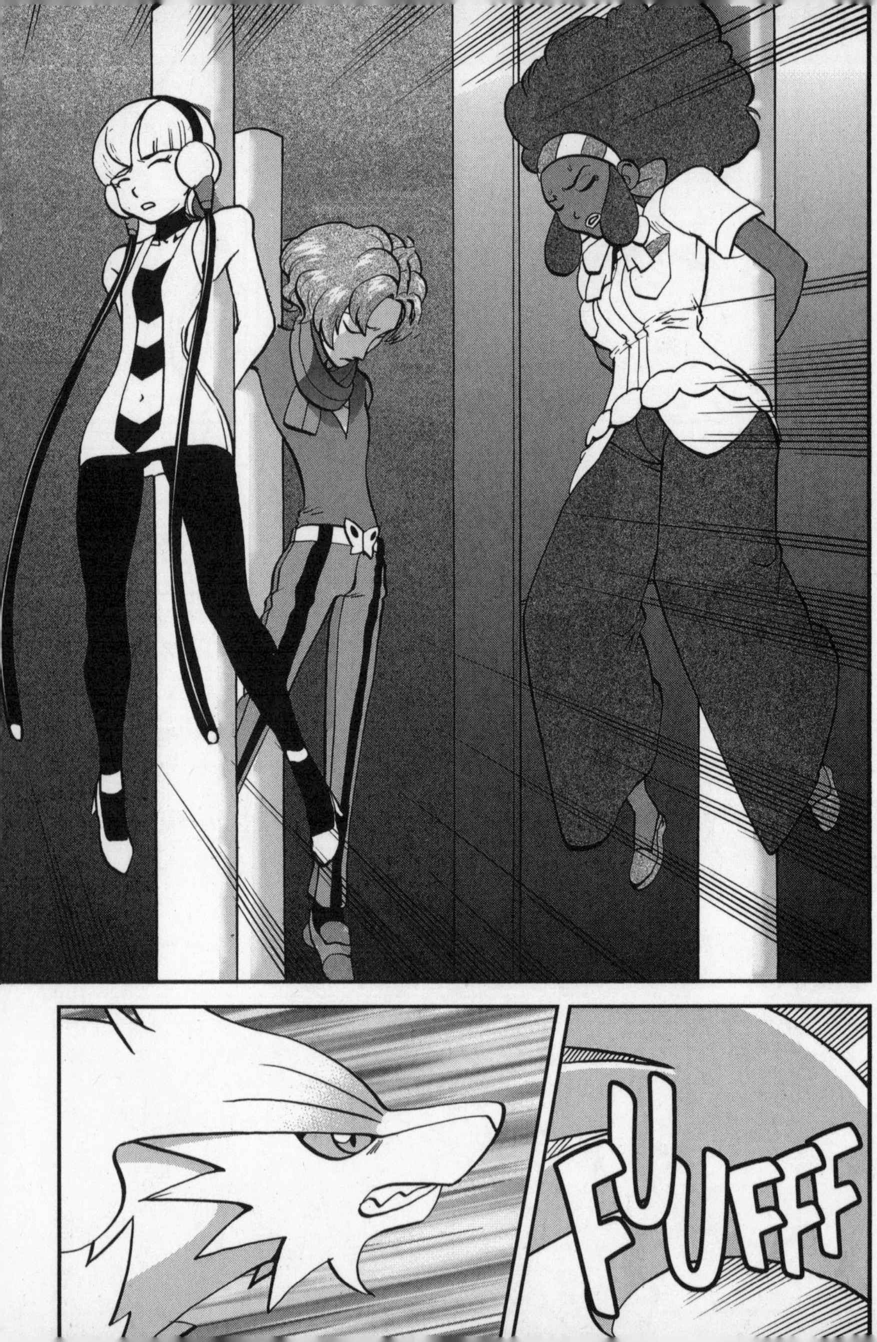
FUUFFF

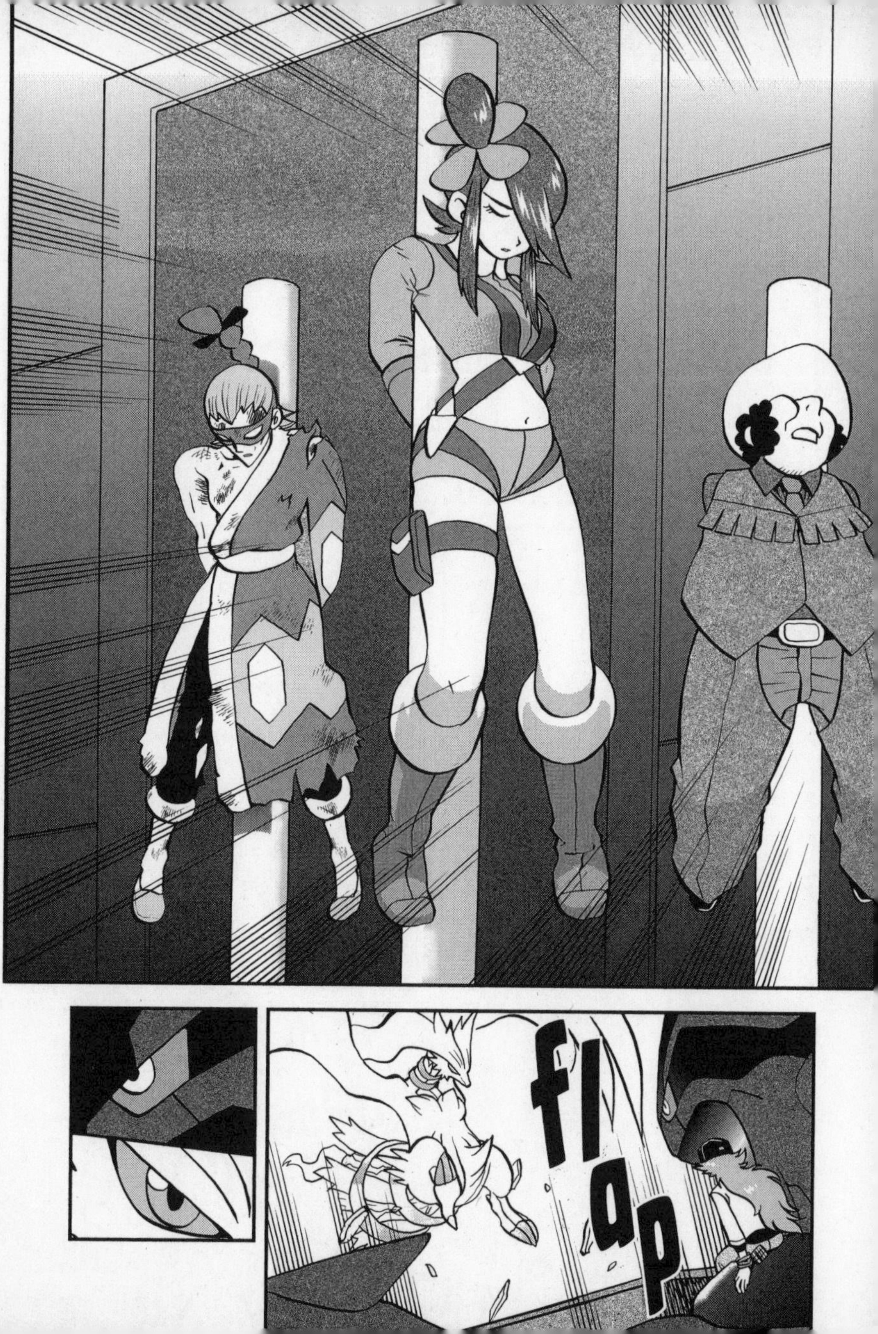
flap

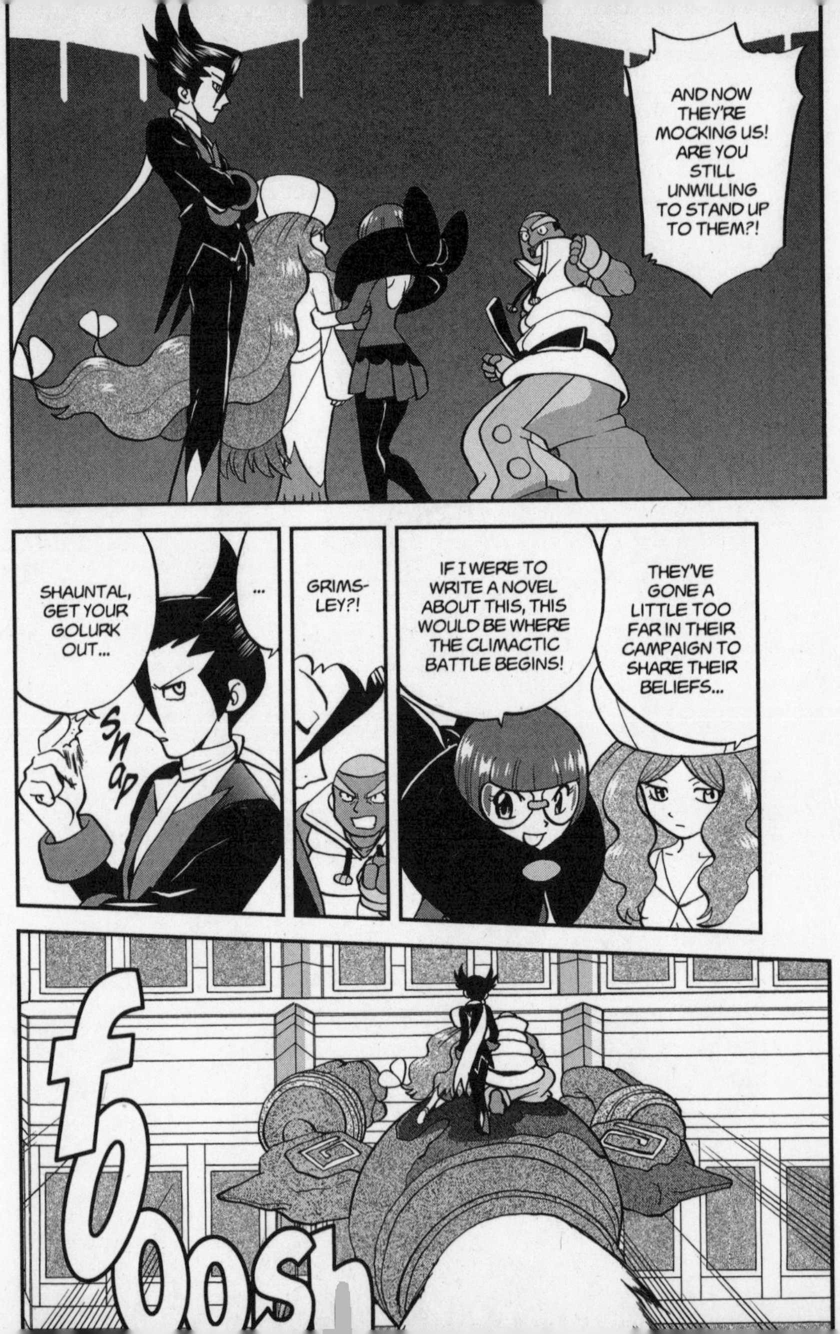
AND NOW THEY'RE MOCKING US! ARE YOU STILL UNWILLING TO STAND UP TO THEM?!
THEY'VE GONE A LITTLE TOO FAR IN THEIR CAMPAIGN TO SHARE THEIR BELIEFS...
IF I WERE TO WRITE A NOVEL ABOUT THIS, THIS WOULD BE WHERE THE CLIMACTIC BATTLE BEGINS!
GRIMS-LEY?!
...
SHAUNTAL, GET YOUR GOLURK OUT...
snap
fooosh

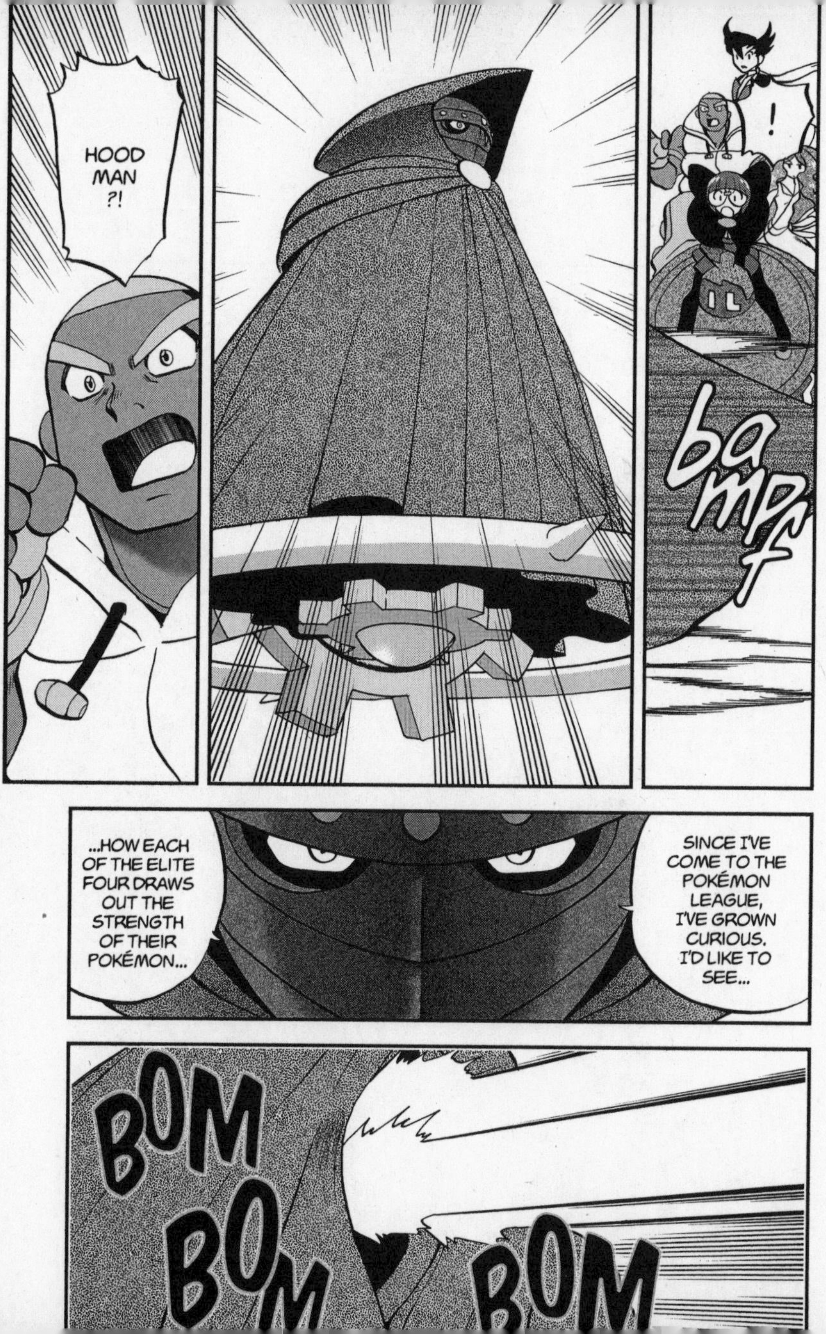
!
bampf
HOOD MAN ?!
SINCE I'VE COME TO THE POKÉMON LEAGUE, I'VE GROWN CURIOUS. I'D LIKE TO SEE...
...HOW EACH OF THE ELITE FOUR DRAWS OUT THE STRENGTH OF THEIR POKÉMON...
BOM
BOM
BOM
BOM

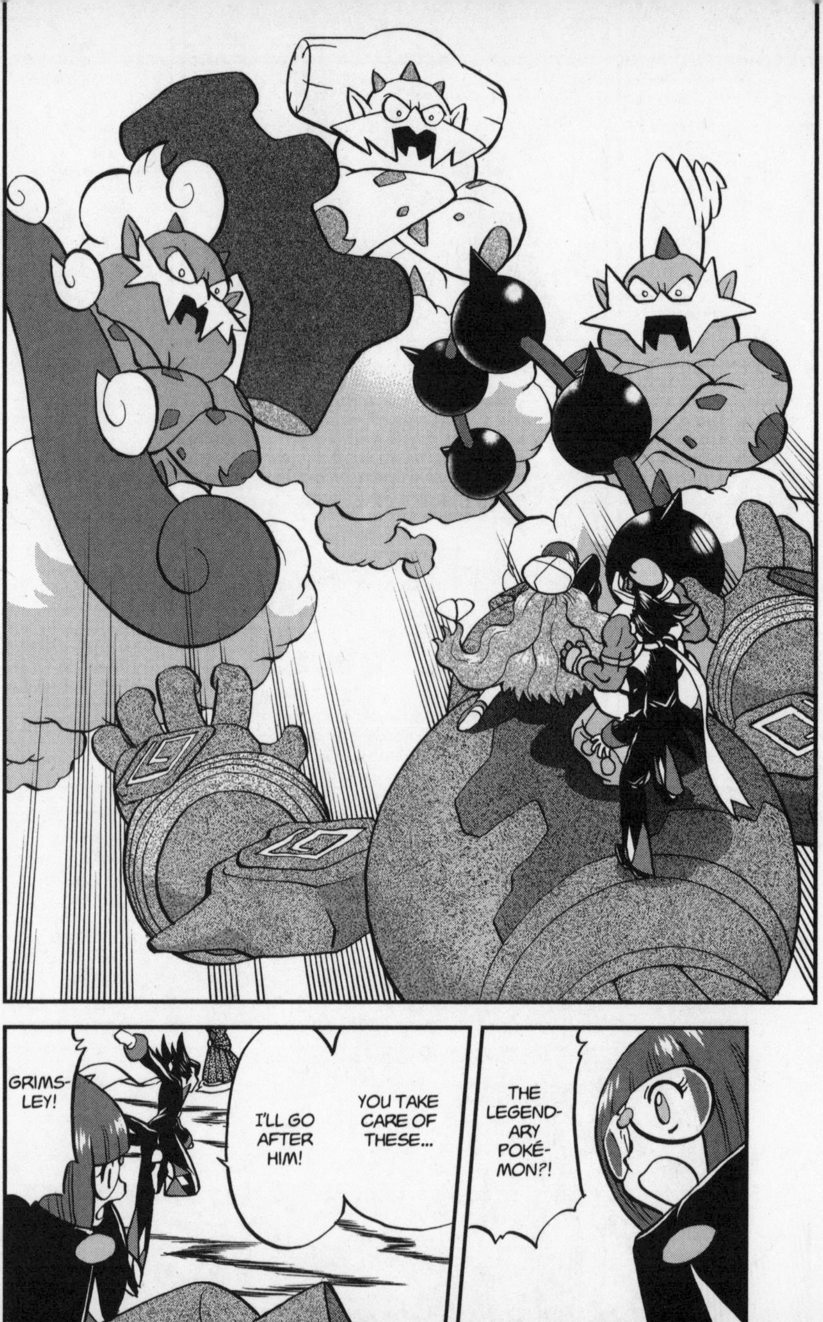
THE LEGENDARY POKÉMON?!
YOU TAKE CARE OF THESE...
I'LL GO AFTER HIM!
GRIMSLEY!

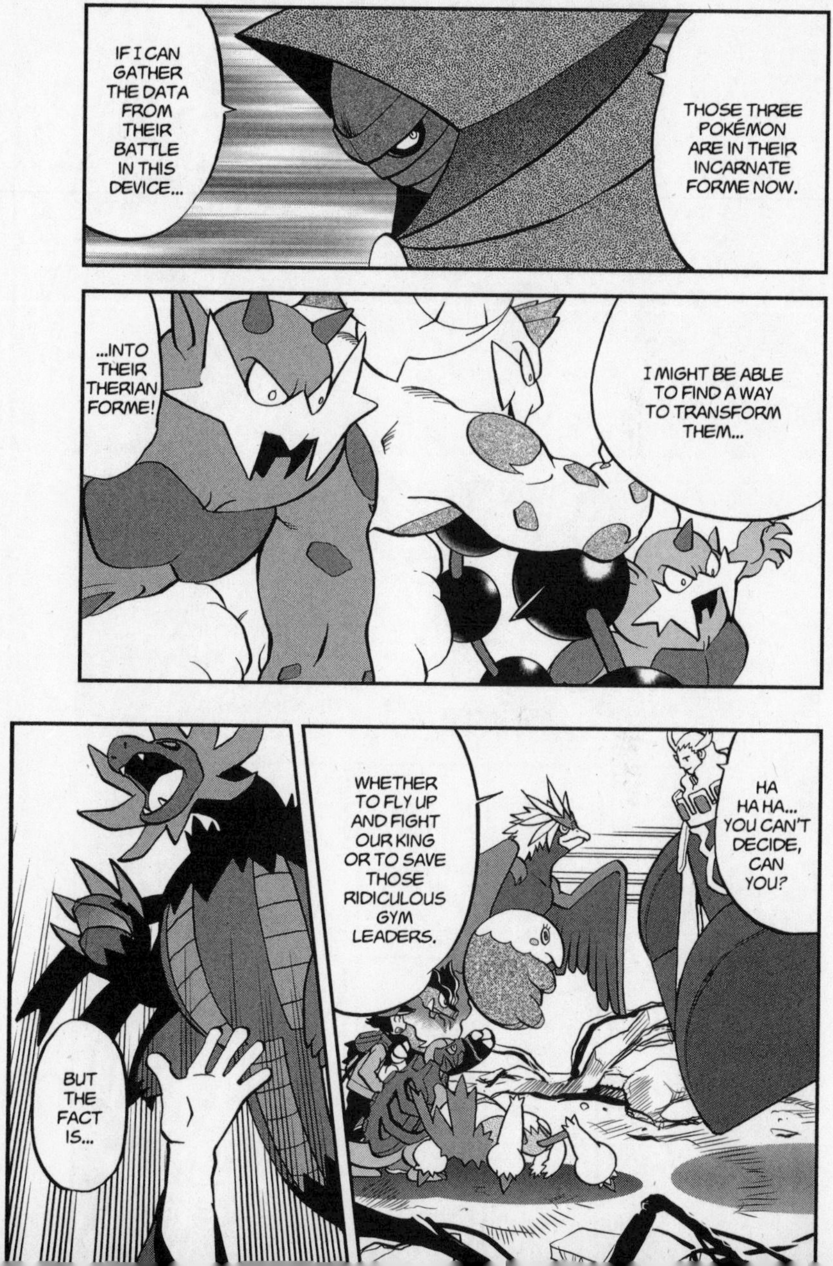
THOSE THREE POKÉMON ARE IN THEIR INCARNATE FORME NOW.
IF I CAN GATHER THE DATA FROM THEIR BATTLE IN THIS DEVICE...
I MIGHT BE ABLE TO FIND A WAY TO TRANSFORM THEM...
...INTO THEIR THERIAN FORME!
HA HA HA... YOU CAN'T DECIDE, CAN YOU?
WHETHER TO FLY UP AND FIGHT OUR KING OR TO SAVE THOSE RIDICULOUS GYM LEADERS.
BUT THE FACT IS...

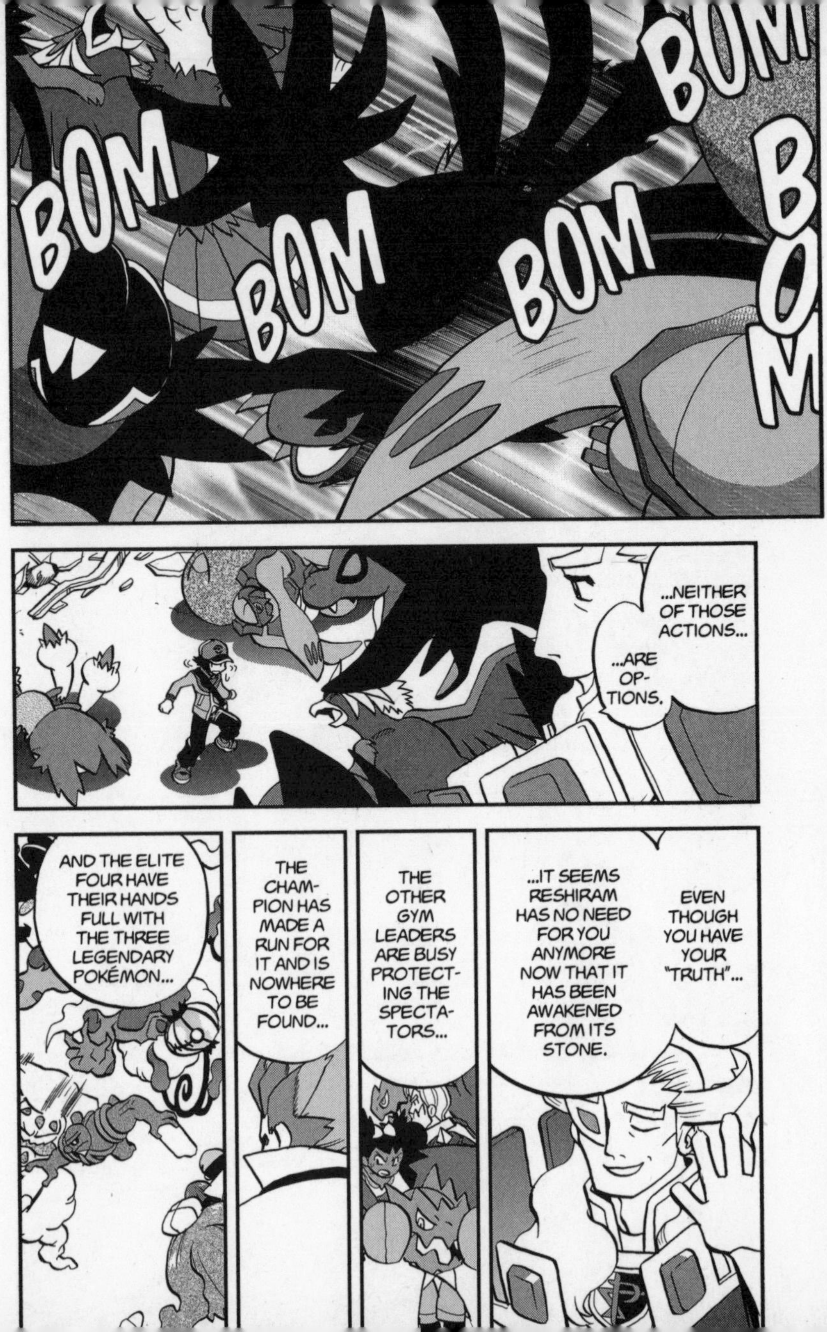
BOM
BOM
BOM
BOM
BOM
...NEITHER OF THOSE ACTIONS...
...ARE OPTIONS.
EVEN THOUGH YOU HAVE YOUR "TRUTH"...
...IT SEEMS RESHIRAM HAS NO NEED FOR YOU ANYMORE NOW THAT IT HAS BEEN AWAKENED FROM ITS STONE.
THE OTHER GYM LEADERS ARE BUSY PROTECTING THE SPECTATORS...
THE CHAMPION HAS MADE A RUN FOR IT AND IS NOWHERE TO BE FOUND...
AND THE ELITE FOUR HAVE THEIR HANDS FULL WITH THE THREE LEGENDARY POKÉMON...

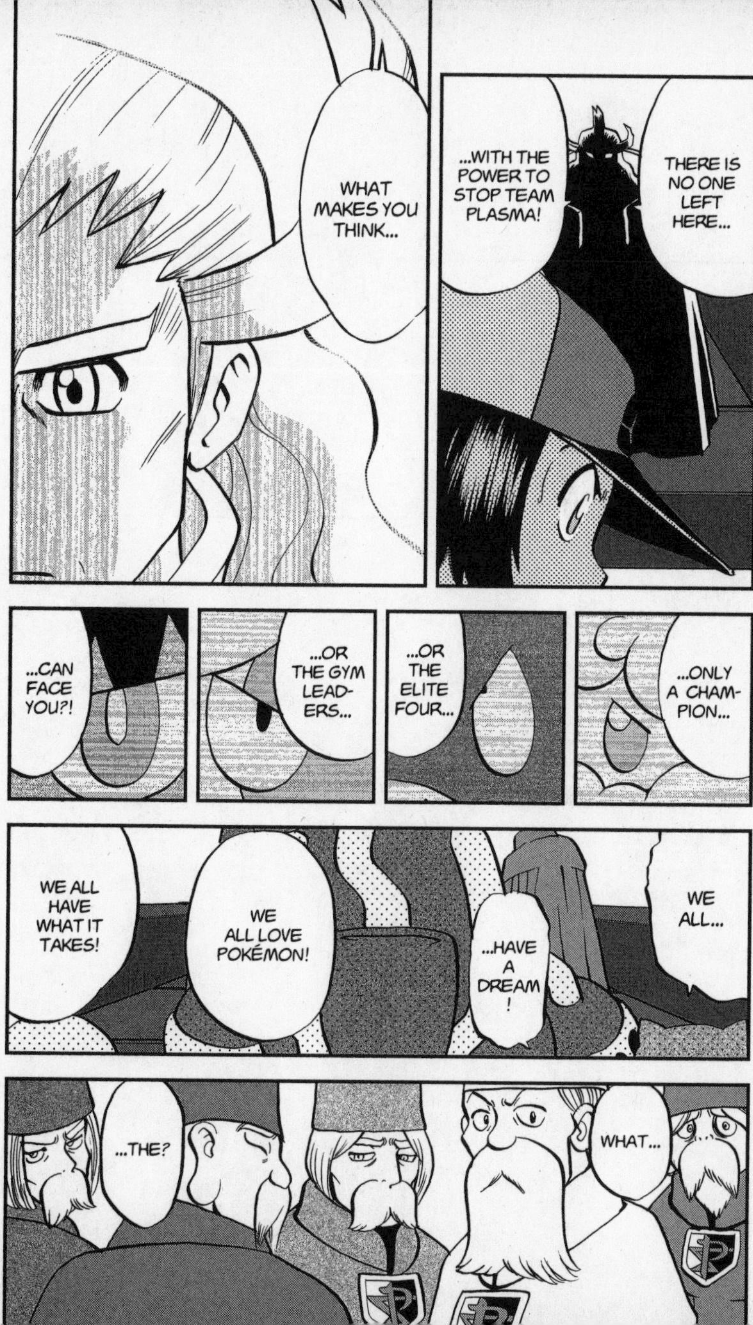
THERE IS NO ONE LEFT HERE...
...WITH THE POWER TO STOP TEAM PLASMA!
WHAT MAKES YOU THINK...
...ONLY A CHAMPION...
...OR THE ELITE FOUR...
...OR THE GYM LEADERS...
...CAN FACE YOU?!
WE ALL...
...HAVE A DREAM!
WE ALL LOVE POKÉMON!
WE ALL HAVE WHAT IT TAKES!
WHAT...
...THE?

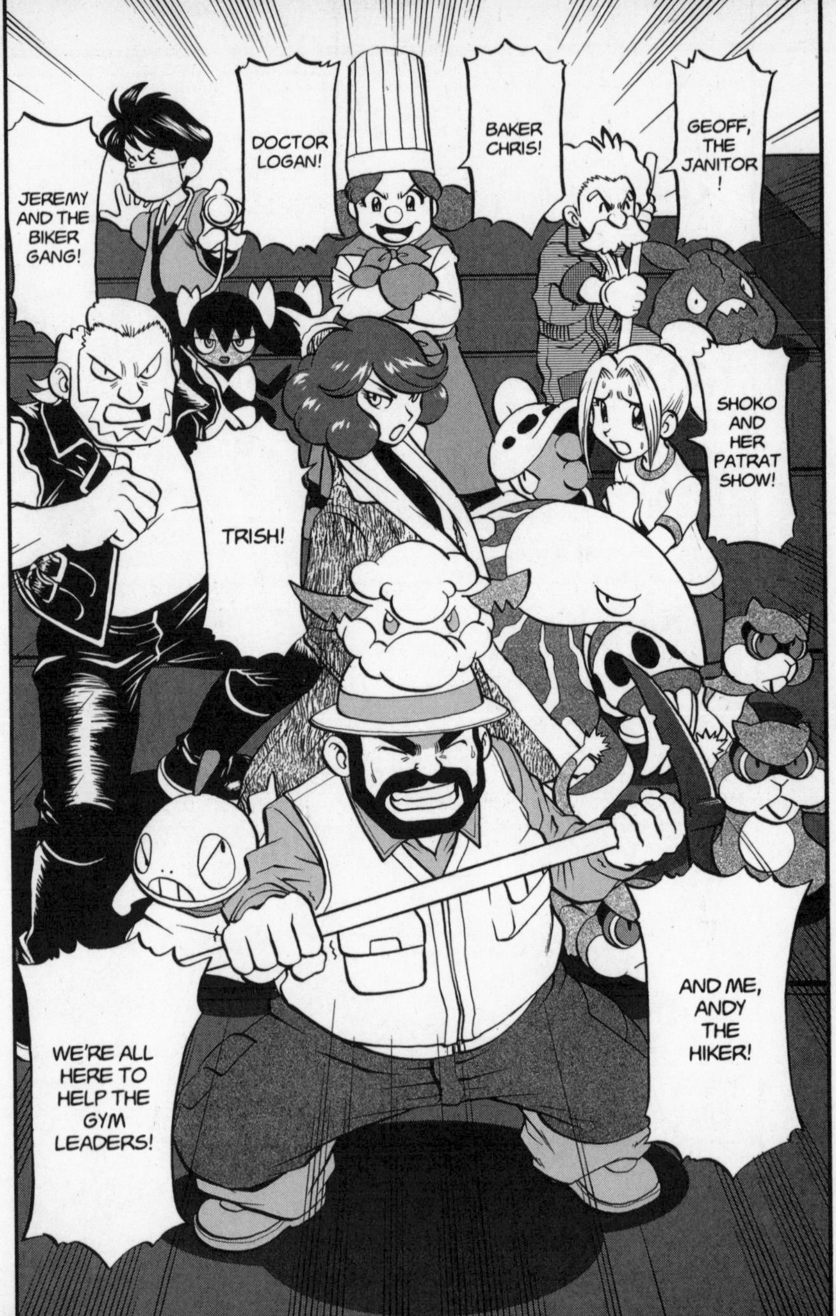
GEOFF, THE JANITOR!
BAKER CHRIS!
DOCTOR LOGAN!
JEREMY AND THE BIKER GANG!
SHOKO AND HER PATRAT SHOW!
TRISH!
AND ME, ANDY THE HIKER!
WE'RE ALL HERE TO HELP THE GYM LEADERS!

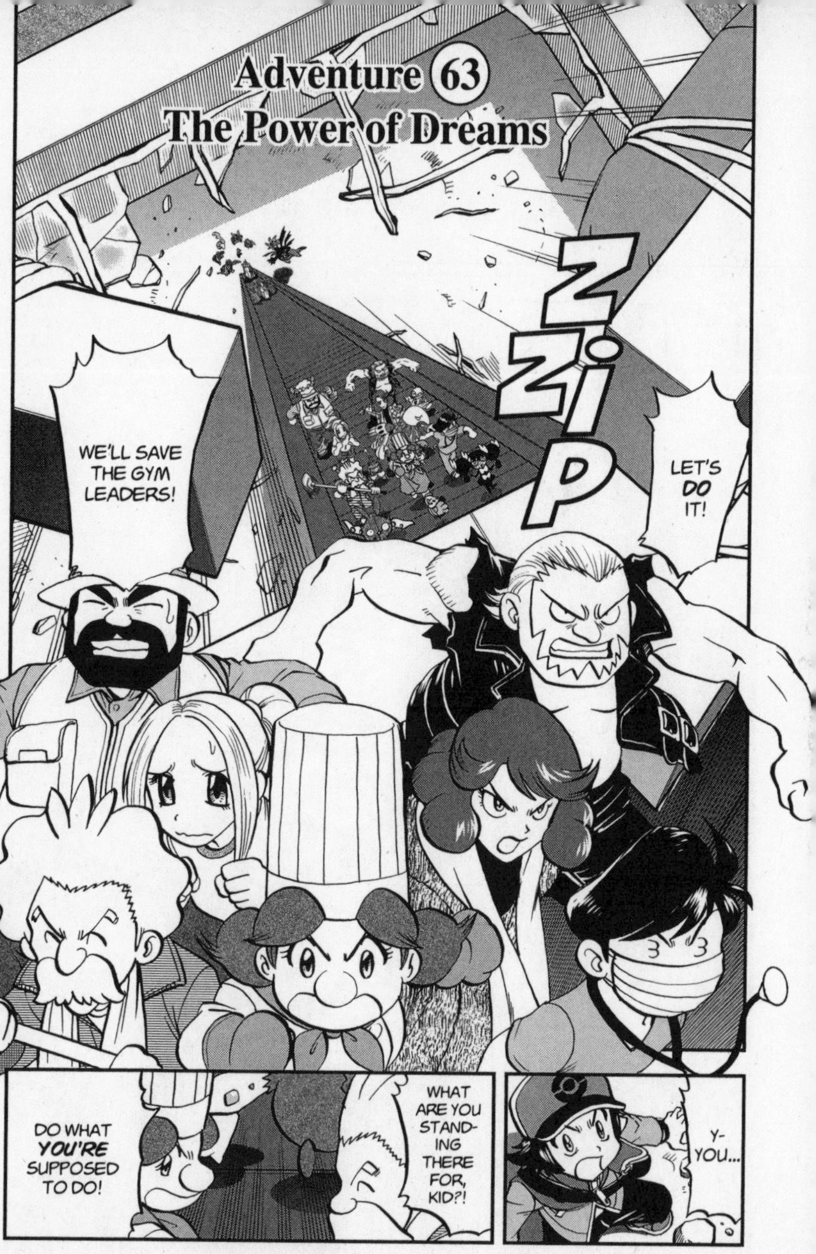
Adventure 63
The Power of Dreams
LET'S DO IT!
ZZIP
WE'LL SAVE THE GYM LEADERS!
Y-YOU...
WHAT ARE YOU STANDING THERE FOR, KID?!
DO WHAT YOU'RE SUPPOSED TO DO!

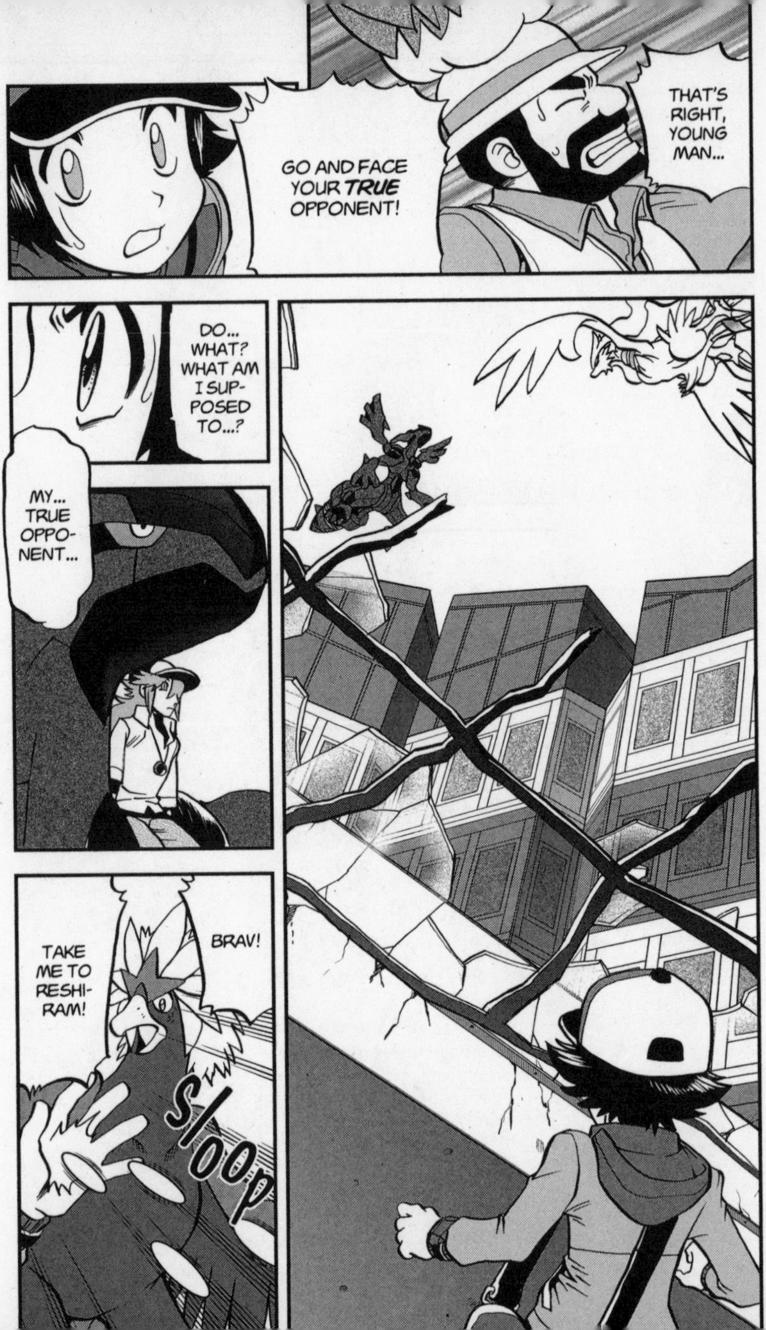
THAT'S RIGHT, YOUNG MAN...
GO AND FACE YOUR TRUE OPPONENT!
DO... WHAT? WHAT AM I SUP-POSED TO...?
MY... TRUE OPPO-NENT...
BRAV!
TAKE ME TO RESHI-RAM!
SLOOP

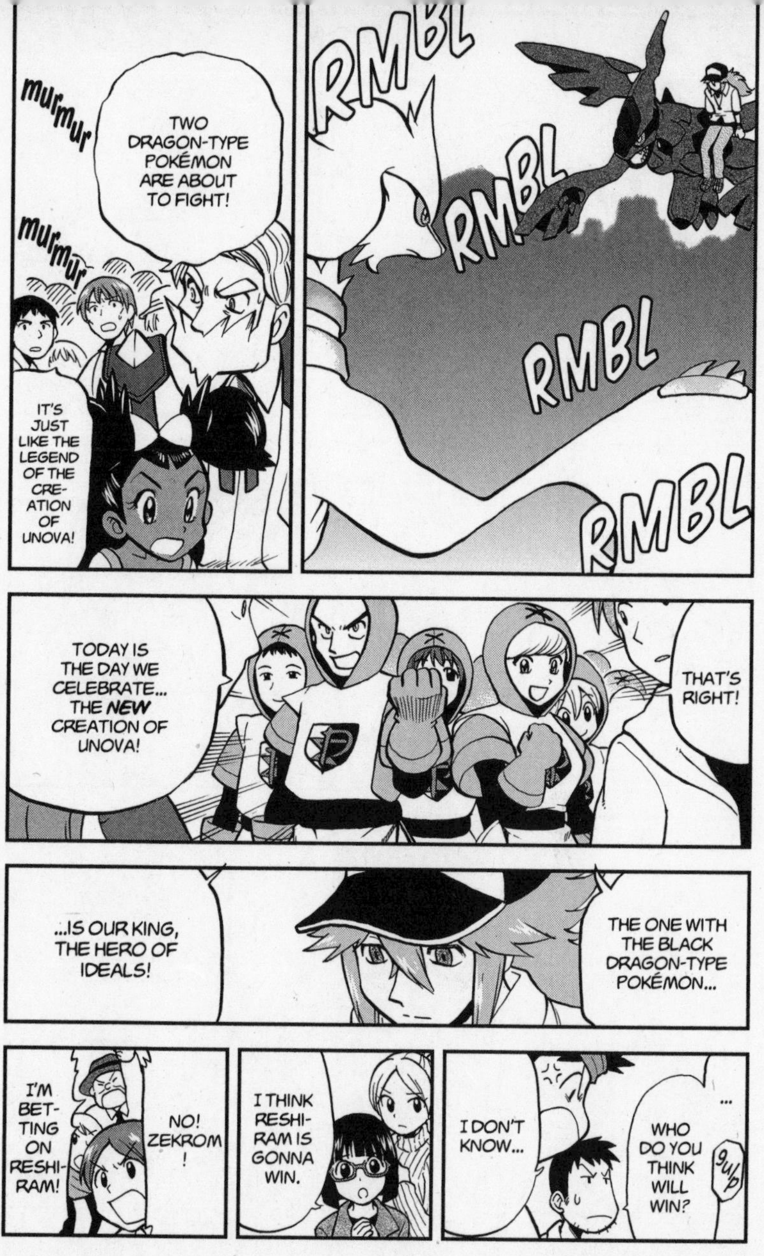
RMBL
RMBL
RMBL
RMBL
RMBL
murmur
TWO DRAGON-TYPE POKÉMON ARE ABOUT TO FIGHT!
murmur
IT'S JUST LIKE THE LEGEND OF THE CRE-ATION OF UNOVA!
THAT'S RIGHT!
TODAY IS THE DAY WE CELEBRATE... THE *NEW* CREATION OF UNOVA!
THE ONE WITH THE BLACK DRAGON-TYPE POKÉMON...
...IS OUR KING, THE HERO OF IDEALS!
...
WHO DO YOU THINK WILL WIN?
gulp
I DON'T KNOW...
I THINK RESHI-RAM IS GONNA WIN.
NO! ZEKROM!
I'M BET-TING ON RESHI-RAM!

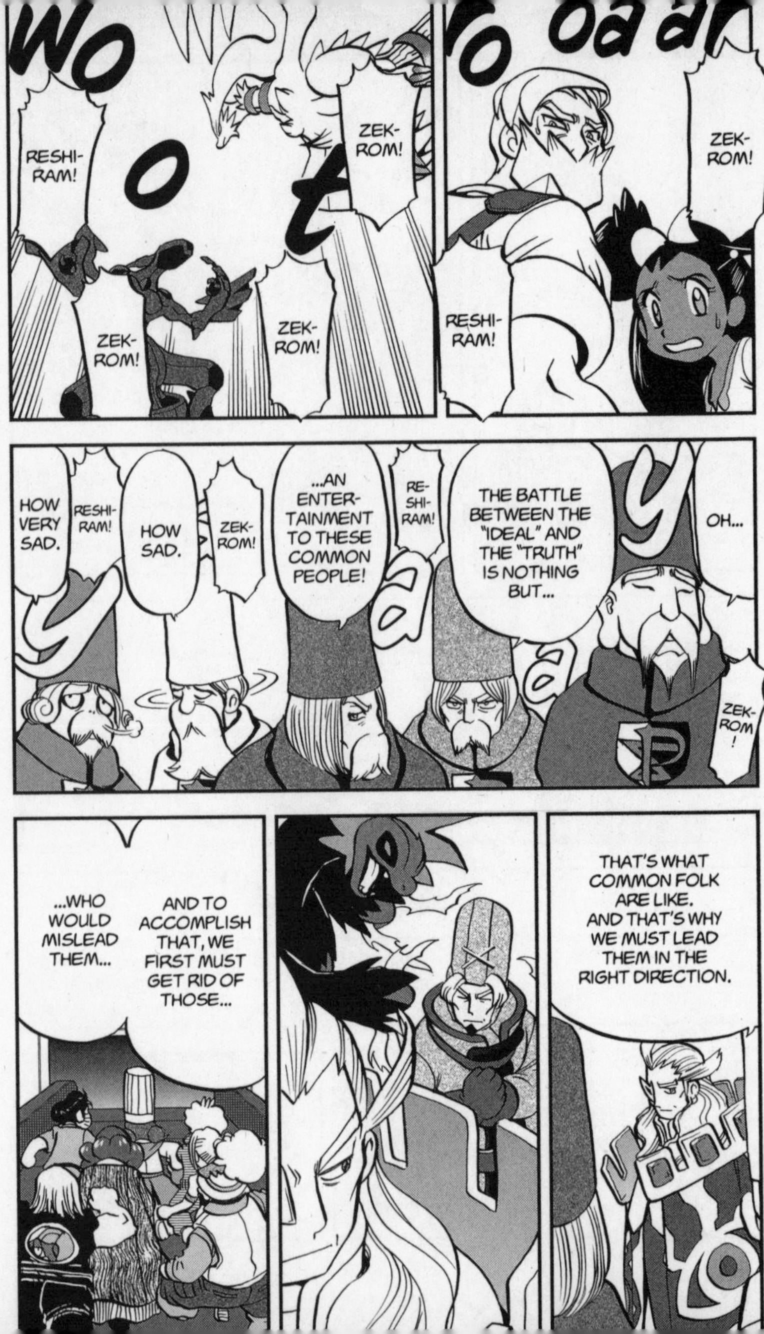
ZEK-ROM!
RESHI-RAM!
ZEK-ROM!
RESHI-RAM!
ZEK-ROM!
ZEK-ROM!
OH...
ZEK-ROM!
THE BATTLE BETWEEN THE "IDEAL" AND THE "TRUTH" IS NOTHING BUT...
RE-SHI-RAM!
...AN ENTER-TAINMENT TO THESE COMMON PEOPLE!
ZEK-ROM!
HOW SAD.
RESHI-RAM!
HOW VERY SAD.
THAT'S WHAT COMMON FOLK ARE LIKE. AND THAT'S WHY WE MUST LEAD THEM IN THE RIGHT DIRECTION.
AND TO ACCOMPLISH THAT, WE FIRST MUST GET RID OF THOSE...
...WHO WOULD MISLEAD THEM...

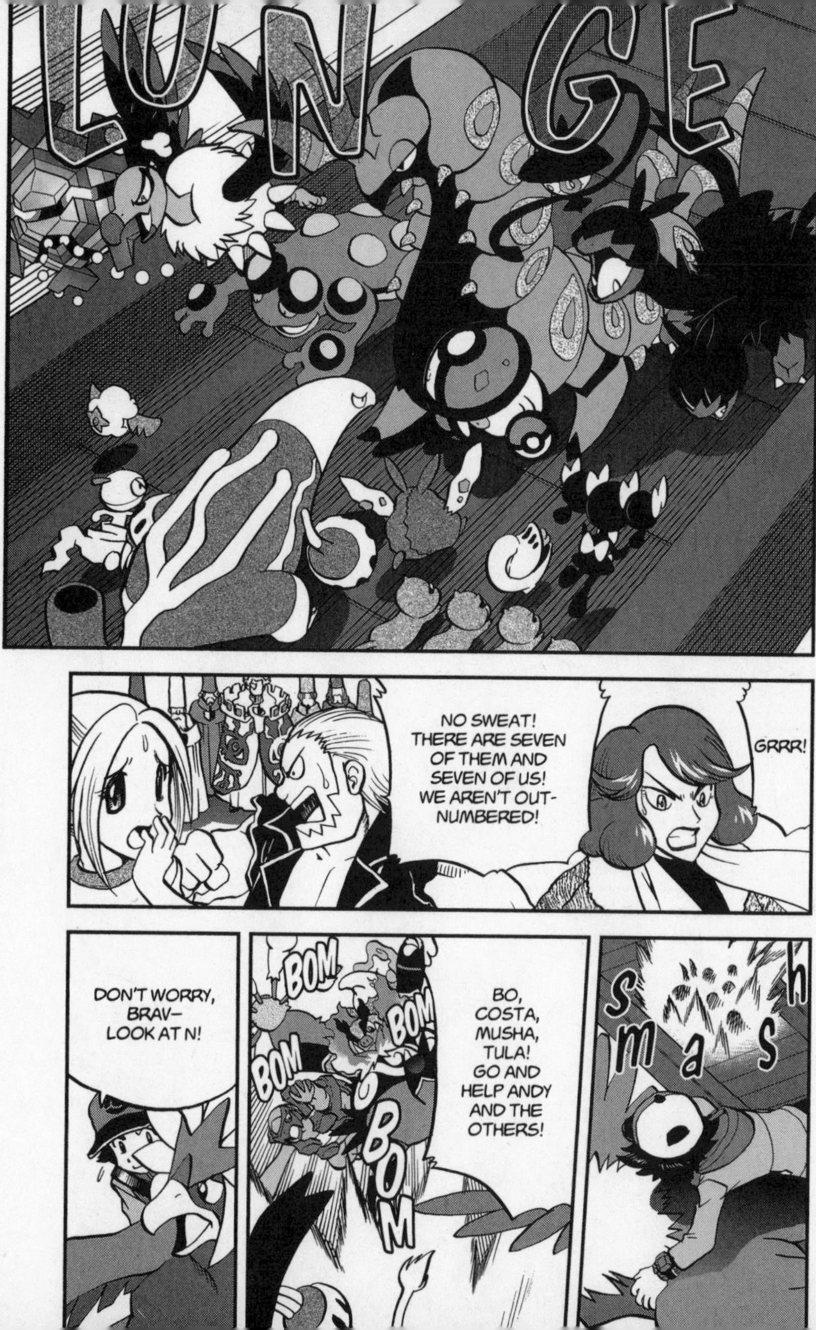
LUNGE
GRRR!
NO SWEAT! THERE ARE SEVEN OF THEM AND SEVEN OF US! WE AREN'T OUT-NUMBERED!
smash
BO, COSTA, MUSHA, TULA! GO AND HELP ANDY AND THE OTHERS!
BOM
BOM
BOM
BOM
DON'T WORRY, BRAV— LOOK AT N!

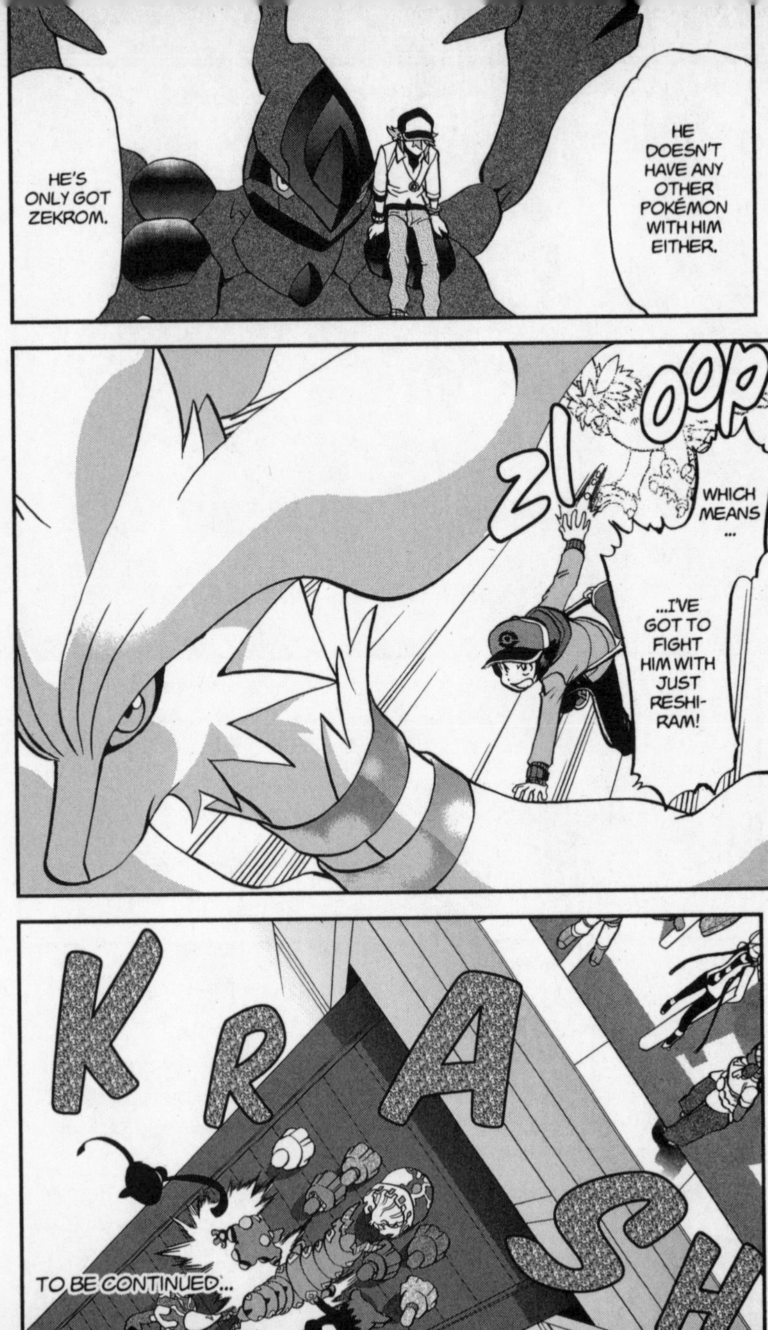
HE DOESN'T HAVE ANY OTHER POKÉMON WITH HIM EITHER.
HE'S ONLY GOT ZEKROM.
ZIOOP
WHICH MEANS ...
...I'VE GOT TO FIGHT HIM WITH JUST RESHI-RAM!
KRASH
TO BE CONTINUED...

More Adventures COMING SOON...

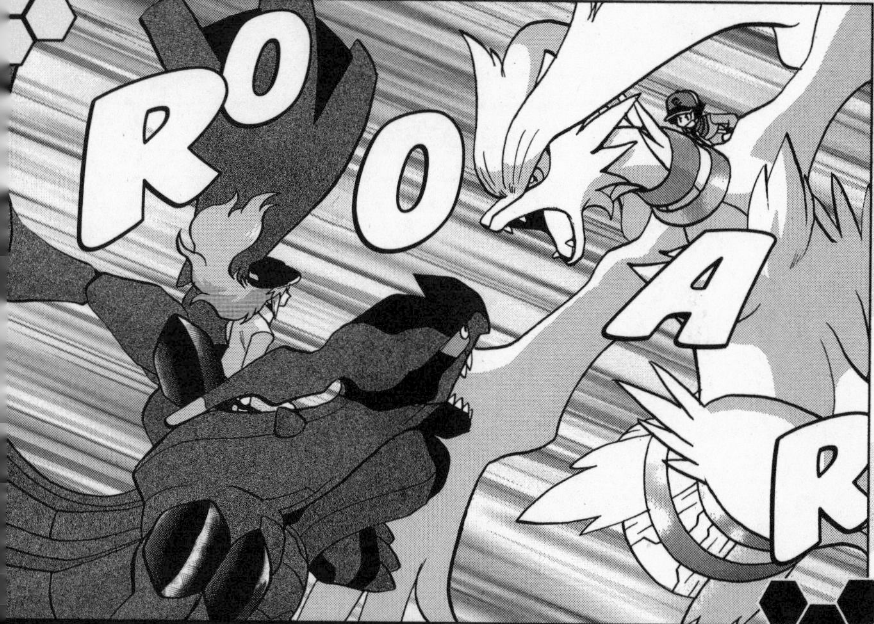
ROOAR

Don't miss the last Pokémon Black and White Special Edition!

Many secrets are finally revealed! Black learns the truth behind Musharna's disappearance. White learns the origin of N, the King of Team Plasma. And the epic battle between Legendary Pokémon Reshiram and Zekrom, wielded by super-skilled Trainers Black and N, rages on... Who will triumph?

AND WHAT IS TEAM PLASMA'S *TRUE* GOAL...?

Plus, watch an all-out battle against Ghetsis's Pokémon team of Hydreigon, Eelektross, Seismitoad, Cofagrigus, and Volcarona!

VOL. 20 AVAILABLE FEBRUARY 2015!

POKÉMON

BLACK & WHITE

STORY & ART BY SANTA HARUKAZE

YOUR FAVORITE POKÉMON FROM THE UNOVA REGION LIKE YOU'VE NEVER SEEN THEM BEFORE!

Available now!

A pocket-sized book brick jam-packed with four-panel comic strips featuring all the Pokémon Black and White characters, Pokémon vital statistics, trivia, puzzles, and fun quizzes!

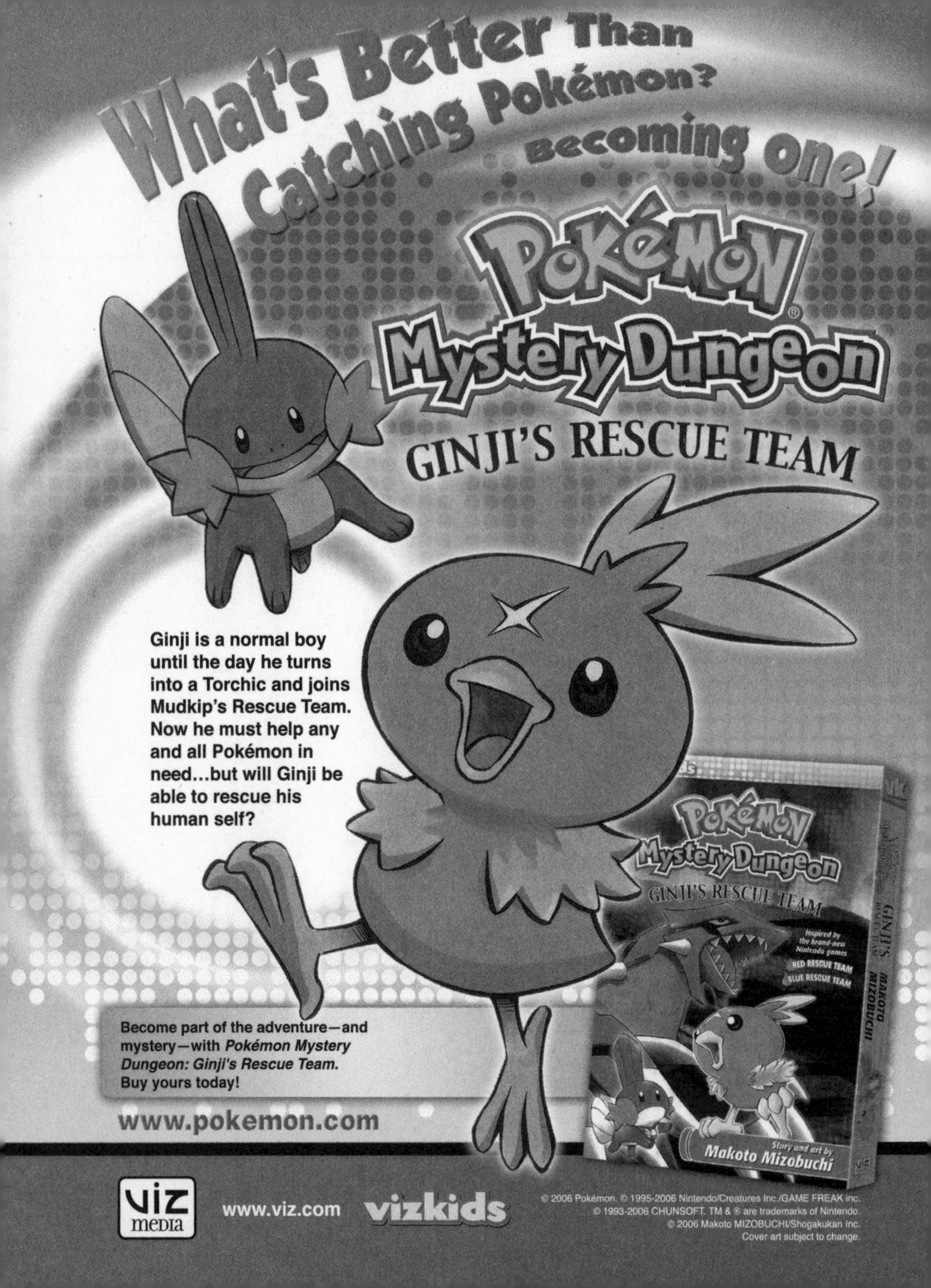
What's Better Than
Catching Pokémon?
Becoming one!
Pokémon®
Mystery Dungeon
GINJI'S RESCUE TEAM
Ginji is a normal boy until the day he turns into a Torchic and joins Mudkip's Rescue Team. Now he must help any and all Pokémon in need...but will Ginji be able to rescue his human self?
Pokémon
Mystery Dungeon
GINJI'S RESCUE TEAM
Inspired by the brand-new Nintendo games
RED RESCUE TEAM
BLUE RESCUE TEAM
GINJI'S RESCUE TEAM
MAKOTO MIZOBUCHI
Story and art by
Makoto Mizobuchi
Become part of the adventure—and mystery—with *Pokémon Mystery Dungeon: Ginji's Rescue Team.* Buy yours today!
www.pokemon.com
viz media
www.viz.com
vizkids
© 2006 Pokémon. © 1995-2006 Nintendo/Creatures Inc./GAME FREAK inc.
© 1993-2006 CHUNSOFT. TM & ® are trademarks of Nintendo.
© 2006 Makoto MIZOBUCHI/Shogakukan Inc.
Cover art subject to change.

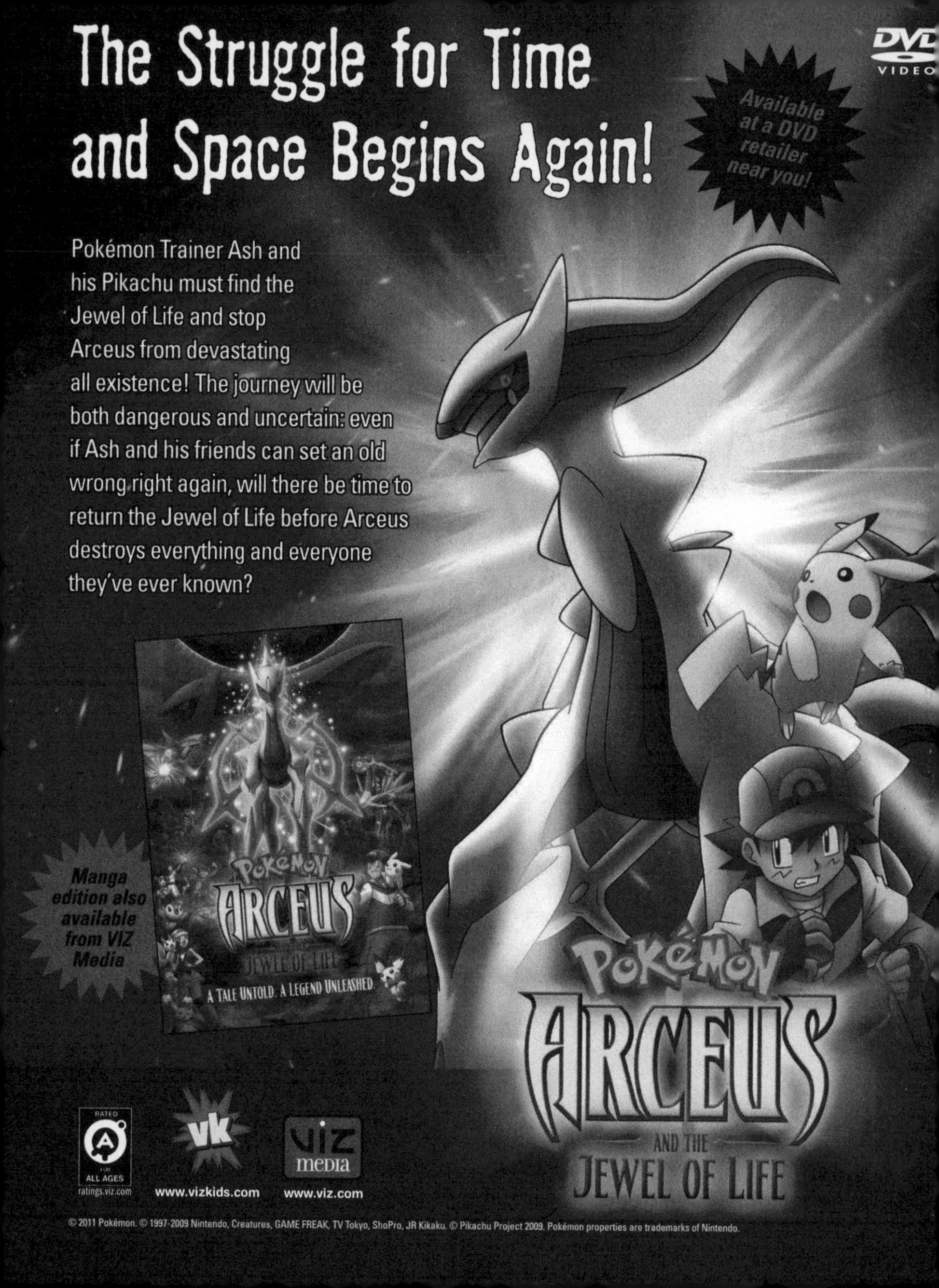
The Struggle for Time
and Space Begins Again!
DVD VIDEO
Available at a DVD retailer near you!
Pokémon Trainer Ash and his Pikachu must find the Jewel of Life and stop Arceus from devastating all existence! The journey will be both dangerous and uncertain: even if Ash and his friends can set an old wrong right again, will there be time to return the Jewel of Life before Arceus destroys everything and everyone they've ever known?
Pokémon Arceus and the Jewel of Life
A Tale Untold. A Legend Unleashed.
Manga edition also available from VIZ Media
Pokémon
Arceus
and the
Jewel of Life
Rated A for All Ages
ratings.viz.com
vk
www.vizkids.com
VIZ media
www.viz.com
© 2011 Pokémon. © 1997-2009 Nintendo, Creatures, GAME FREAK, TV Tokyo, ShoPro, JR Kikaku. © Pikachu Project 2009. Pokémon properties are trademarks of Nintendo.

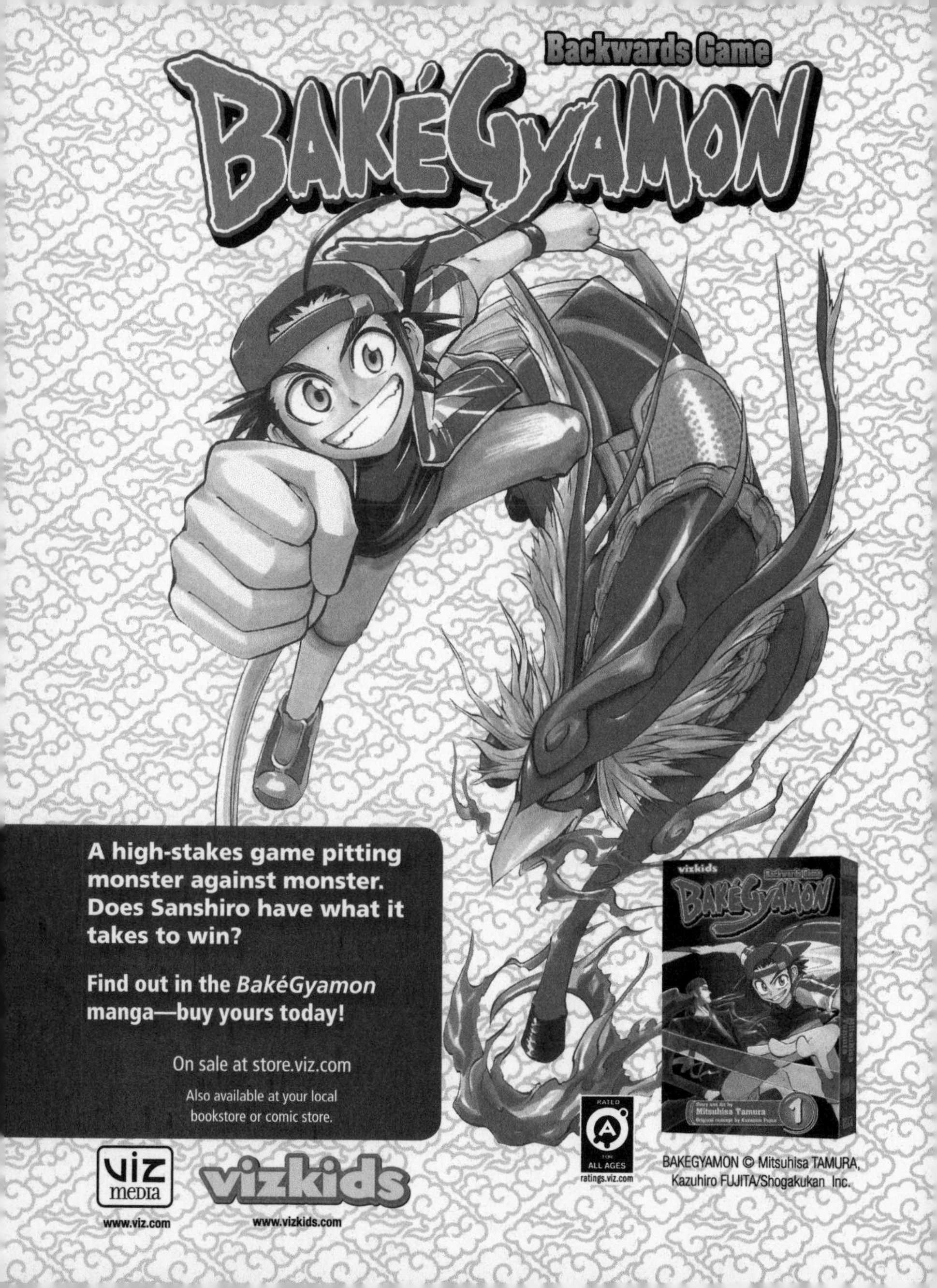
Backwards Game
BAKÉGYAMON

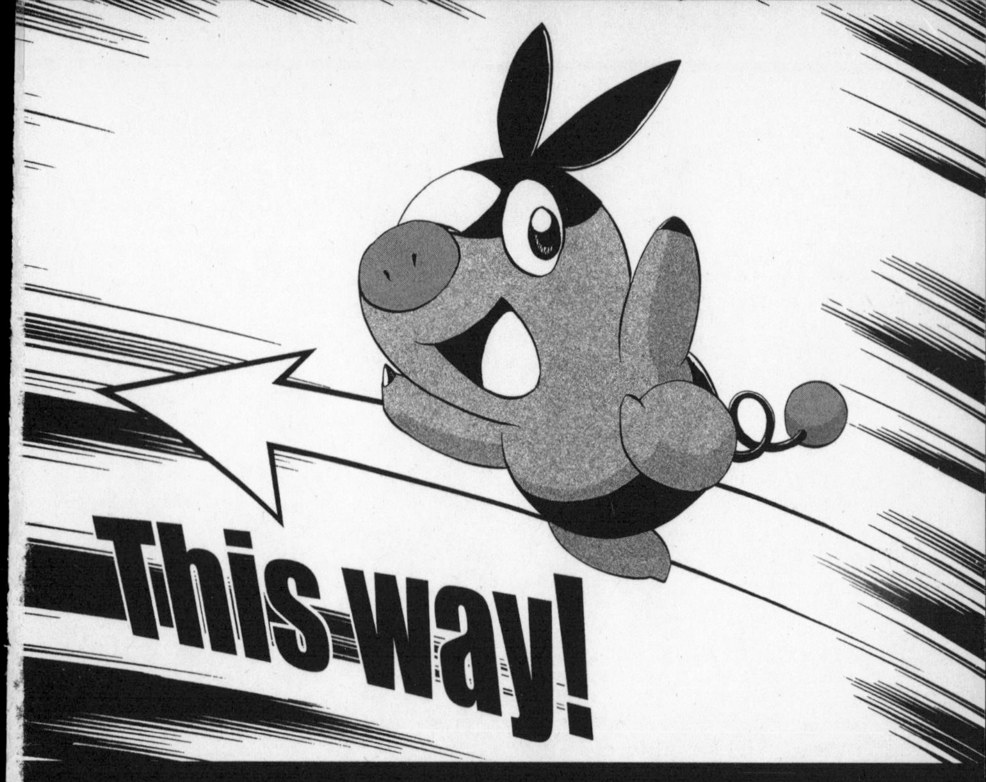
This way!

THIS IS THE END OF THIS GRAPHIC NOVEL!

To properly enjoy this VIZ Media graphic novel, please turn it around and begin reading from right to left.

This book has been printed in the original Japanese format in order to preserve the orientation of the original artwork. Have fun with it!

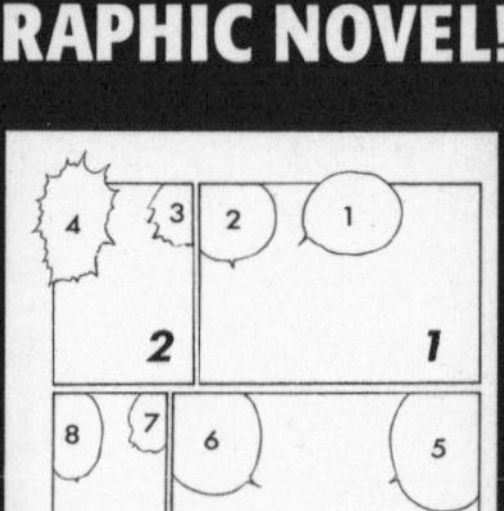
1
2
3
4
1
2
5
6
7
8
3
4
9
5
142
follow the action this way.

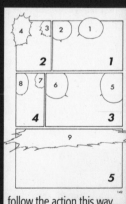